CW00684043

CATCHEE MONKEY

A REX & EDDIE MYSTERY

SEAN CAMERON

DAPPER FOX
PUBLISHING

Cover Design: Anthony S. Hales

ISBN: 1946215023
ISBN-13: 978-1946215024

Copyright © 2014 by Sean Cameron
All rights reserved.

No part of this book may be reproduced in any form or by any electronic or mechanical means, including information storage and retrieval systems, without written permission from the author, except for the use of brief quotations in a book review.

PROLOGUE

"Cloisterham, an OK place to live." That was the town's actual slogan. Eight years ago a disgruntled employee slipped it past the local council's review, and the slogan was printed on every road sign, public building, and all official stationery.

Due to budget restrictions, the council waited until the next year to fix it; even then the new stationery had to run out before they adopted a new slogan. Since the majority of the town's population grew accustomed to the motto, it was changed to the equally true "Cloisterham, a place to live."

The town centre had a postcard-worthy Victorian high street. The bricked road was lined with wonky historic shops next to a well-preserved medieval castle and the second oldest cathedral in England. Beyond that lay a sprawling urban collection of neighbourhoods. Some seemed quite palatable, but Cloisterham had its fair share of roads it would be best to avoid walking down.

Harold, a simple cleaner waiting for retirement, lived on a road no-one wanted to walk down, but he worked on the high street, the industrial end not the postcard-pretty end. He liked the town's slogan because it was simple and direct, which he always appreciated. Harold took the cleaner job because the description was short and clear, plus it was such little work for the money he felt like a thief.

Silly buggers, he thought.

369 High Street was four Georgian houses joined together to create a makeshift office rental space. It was a pretty cramped space with narrow stairs and a thin corridor. The tenants would grumble about the space, but for Harold, it meant there was less to clean. He'd sweep the stairs, mop the floor, clean the bathrooms, and empty the wastepaper baskets on a daily basis. When a tenant moved out, Harold would give the office a deep clean, at the expense of their deposit, of course.

Dirty buggers, he thought.

Every morning, Harold was the first one in the building, until one Tuesday when he found an office door left ajar and the light on. He approached the unit and pushed the door open. On the floor lay a body with half a head. The other half was sprayed across the hardwood floors and up the wall. Although his contract never explicitly stated so, Harold knew the clean up would be his job.

Bugger, he thought.

When it came to the police report, he also described a sprinkling of brains across the desk. Harold wasn't suggesting the brains had been deliberately sprinkled across the desk, he was sure they just landed there. He just liked it when cooking shows added an ingredient and called it a "sprinkling."

The police asked Harold if he'd seen anything else. He mentioned the "dash" of teeth in the corner.

"Did you see anyone come in or out that could have done this?" the Detective Inspector said.

Harold shrugged his shoulders. “Nope.”
“Did you know the victim?”
“Not well.”
“Can you tell us anything about him?”
“I know he won’t be getting his deposit back.”

ONE

Being short in stature, though not enough that anyone noticed straightaway, Eddie Miles never forgot to wear his hat to work. At The Octagon Shopping Centre, a rundown building filled with discount stores and knock-off shops, it was important to give off an air of authority.

The other security guards didn't have his prim and proper nature, but Eddie felt it was his duty to look like an imposing foe to the potential shoplifter. The peaked security cap helped. It was the tactic of the blowfish, but Eddie wasn't ashamed; after all, it worked for the blowfish. He only took the hat off for lunch breaks with his girlfriend, Melinda.

On his lunch hour, he collected Melinda and grabbed a Scotch egg at the bakery. She was a petite girl with a go get 'em attitude. She sold shoes at The Octagon, which was perfect for her because she was decisive. She picked shoes that helped people make a statement about themselves. Eddie and Melinda sat on a bench, and she took a bite of her tuna sandwich.

She gave a deep sigh. "Eddie, I can't do this anymore."

"It's okay, it's dolphin-friendly tuna."

"No. This. Us."

"You don't like to take lunch breaks together?"

"I don't think we should do anything together. I think we should break up."

Eddie chewed and swallowed his Scotch egg. He hated to talk with his mouth full, no matter how awkward the wait was.

"You want to break up? Why?"

"You're not going anywhere."

"Oh, phew." Eddie motioned a wipe of his brow. "I thought you were getting rid of me."

"You're not making me feel heard. I am getting rid of you."

"What? Why?"

"I'm an assistant manager now, but you, you're a security guard. You're not doing anything with your life. I need an exciting go-getter. I need someone that's going places. Look at your shoes, they're not the shoes of someone going places. They are square, dull shoes."

"You said they were perfect for me."

"They are."

"You're breaking up with me because of my shoes?"

"It's what they represent. You never take any risks. You never surprise me. You even eat the same lunch every day. You never want to go out. Its like, you're boring, you don't really have a sense of humour, your voice is a bit annoying—"

"All right, all right, I understand. I'm not going anywhere."

"And you're boring and—"

"Thanks, Melinda. I get it."

After lunch, Eddie joined Rex on the mezzanine floor and watched over the shoppers. Rex Milton was shaggy-haired and sported round glasses, his light step and playful smiles gave off a friendly, child-like innocence. He was six-foot-tall without a hat, but shoplifters weren't scared of him.

Eddie ranted about his break-up, but Rex was so interested in a muddy footprint he didn't hear a word, and crouched to inspect the print. Noticing he'd lost Rex's attention, Eddie wondered if he really was boring.

"Rex, get up, you'll get us into trouble."

"Today's the day, Eddie. Today we solve the mystery and find the culprit with the muddy shoes. From this day on, they will warn others of the time they were busted for making weekly visits without wiping their boots at the door."

"No, it's not. Today is the day we stand here with no trouble."

"Trouble is everywhere, Eddie. You're just not as observant as me."

Eddie scoffed. "You're joking."

"I wanted to stop that shoplifter the other day, and you wouldn't let me because you didn't see it."

"Because the shop didn't see it. Unless they report it to us, over the radio, our orders are to stand here."

"And watch them leave with their loot?"

"The watching is optional."

Rex sulked.

"Sorry, Rex. Unless it's reported, we have to wait for them to steal something out here in the walkway."

"But all the stuff is in the shops. This is boring."

"You're telling me. By the end of my first day, I was bored enough to count the sides of the building."

"Eight, duh. That's why it's called The Octagon Shopping Centre."

"If you count them, it's actually seven."

Rex's forehead furrowed. "So why is it called The Octagon?"

"It's a mystery. I've asked around, but no one knows. My theory is the owners realised nobody knows what a heptagon is."

"What's a heptagon?"

Eddie sighed. "Never mind."

"You're right, it's a rubbish mystery. No chase, no suspense, no femme fatale."

"Femme fatales don't live in a town like Cloisterham. As for fast car chases, you'd be lucky to reach thirty miles an hour in rush hour."

Rex was adamant he'd solve a crime one day. At this point in time, finding the offender with the muddy footprints suited his needs. After sticking his finger in the mud, Rex sniffed his hand and licked it.

Eddie grimaced. "Why would you do that?"

"I saw it in a movie."

"It's disgusting."

"I thought it might lead to another clue."

"Stop it, Rex. A dirty floor has nothing to do with us."

"It's a form of vandalism. I'm so close to finding the perpetrator. I've been to all the shoe stores and narrowed it down to two possible boot footprint patterns."

"You need to stop."

"Both footprints are only available at Melinda's shoe shop. We know where they buy footwear."

"I don't want to talk about Melinda or the shoe shop. Plus, they've already bought the boots. You've found the one shop they don't need to go in."

"Oh, right. Well, they'll still need shoe polish."

Eddie observed the muddy print. "I don't think they care about how clean the boots are."

"Come on Eddie, this is important, we have to up our game, take on the uber-criminal. Be uber-secure. Could be an uber-pay rise in it."

Uber was Rex's word of the day. He'd hear a new word from time to time, usually from his friend Jim Jams, and shoehorn it into as many conversations as possible. It mostly irritated Eddie, other times he learnt something new, not that he'd admit it.

"Stand up, will you."

"Fine, I don't need the boot print," Rex said. "I can tell who's a crook or not with my gut instinct."

"Okay, what about those two?" Eddie pointed at a fragile old lady confused by the shopping centre map, and a hooded teenage boy who skulked about the mezzanine.

"Obvious. It's the old lady."

"Is that your final answer?"

"Of course, what else does she need a big bag for? I bet it's for stealing."

"I'll bet you ten quid?"

"Done."

They shook on it. As Rex marched towards the poor woman, Eddie realised what a mistake he'd made, and all the blood left his head.

"Rex, no. Please. Stay. Stay!"

Rex tapped the poor pensioner on the shoulder. "Sorry to bother you, madam." Eddie ran between them. "Excuse me, Eddie, I'm talking to the elderly lady."

The old woman dropped her jaw. "I beg your pardon?"

"Her hearing must be going." Rex shouted, "I will need to check your bag, madam."

She tightened her grasp, pulling the bag to her chest. "Why?"

"Just give us a look."

"I will do no such thing."

Rex delved his arm into her bag. She wrestled it away until Rex pulled out a prescription bottle.

"What's this? Drugs? Pushing pills on my turf, are we?"

"It's medicine, she's not a drug dealer."

Rex snatched the bag from the fuming old woman. "Semi-retired perhaps."

Eddie yanked the bag from Rex. "Just give it back to her."

They both tugged back and forth until Rex let go. Eddie pulled so hard he fell back on his backside. The bag flung across the walkway. The hooded teen spotted earlier scooped the bag up and bolted.

"Oi," Eddie shouted.

The pair jumped up and sprinted after the thief.

The hooded thief rushed past a shop display and knocked it over. Toys spilt all over the floor. Rex and Eddie navigated themselves around the falling debris, but Eddie slipped on a Magic 8 ball and crashed into a skateboard display. As the Magic 8 ball rolled passed Eddie's head the display read, *Outlook not so good.*

Rex leapt over Eddie and jumped on a rolling skateboard. His right foot propelled him towards the teen. Rex gained on the little thief and reached out his hand. He was inches away from grabbing his target's hood. Eddie thought it was most impressive until the teen made a sharp turn and escaped.

Too fast to turn, Rex glided straight towards an open lift. The occupants jumped out of his way as Rex whacked into the elevator's back wall. He turned around confused as the lift doors closed on him. Rex was gone.

Eddie jumped to his feet and ran. The thief bashed

through a fire exit and darted up a stairwell. Eddie cramped up on the stairs, he was out of breath and ready to puke. The teen had already made it up one flight.

"If you surrender—" Eddie's voice came out a little too high-pitch, so he cleared his throat, which made him dry heave. "If you surrender now, we'll go lightly on you."

Silence. The teen stopped.

Eddie stood tall and proud. He leant forward over the bannister to check for the teen's reaction. A crystal ball flew down and hit Eddie on the head.

"Ouch!" Eddie stomped around in a circle as if it had some sort of beneficial purpose.

A crystal ball? he thought. *The little git must have stolen it from the mystic shop.*

Eddie didn't believe in that mystical stuff, but somehow the crystal ball's energy empowered him, or maybe the adrenaline kicked in.

Stolen objects continued to rain down as Eddie navigated up the stairs with speed and focus. Nothing could stop him, not a flying tin of beans, not an onslaught of kitchen tools, not even another dreaded Magic 8 ball.

Eddie followed the perpetrator into the car parking structure. His legs wobbled, and the stitches in his side tightened. He tried to catch up but fell to his knees.

This isn't how a twenty-eight-year-old's body is meant to behave, he thought.

In Eddie's moment of defeat, the teen sprinted past an opening elevator door. Rex rode out on the skateboard. He pushed the skateboard along and chased the teen. Eddie painfully pumped his fist with pride, but mostly pain.

Once again, Rex headed towards victory until a car drove between him and the thief. Rex rode straight into the car's side while the skateboard slid under the vehicle. The vehicle sped off as Rex fell on his back. Rex rolled over to face Eddie. They both gave each other an apologetic half-smile as the thief reached the exit's white light.

The hooded teen ran towards the exit barriers until the skateboard — which continued to chase after the teen — slid under the running criminal as he lowered his right foot. The speeding skateboard pulled the teen's right leg forward, and he lunged further than any male should. The hoodie fell forward as he dropped the stolen bag, which spun across the floor and threw its contents out like a carousel firework. Mouth agape, the teen fell on his side against the concrete floor.

Eddie staggered to Rex, and they both hobbled over to the teen. They could not assess the teen's state, but his jeans were split. Rex and Eddie checked out the scattered bag items: a can of soup, an incense candle, a pack of electric toothbrush heads, and some DVDs in their original wrapper. It seemed the old lady was a shoplifter.

Rex smiled. "You owe me a tenner."

TWO

A spongy leather seat never felt so uncomfortable to Eddie. He shuffled in the chair as the amount of company rules the pair broke bounced around in Eddie's swollen head. Technically, they weren't supposed to chase thieves once they got into the parking structure. At that point, they were meant to call the police. Their job really was just standing.

The manager sat across his desk giving Rex and Eddie a stare down. His name was Albert Griffin. Eddie always called him Mr Griffin. Chief is what Rex called him. He thought Griffin was the head of security, so he treated him like the chief of police.

Rex gave a salute. "Reporting for duty, Chief."

"Sit down, Rex," Griffin barked in his gruff voice.

Griffin had grey curly hair and wore the same two old suits on alternating workdays. In his late fifties, he'd worked enough years behind a desk to know he didn't like it. Griffin now glided towards early retirement and spent his workdays making ships in a bottle.

Eddie flinched at any sign of Griffin opening his

mouth; he fully anticipated a verbal onslaught. Griffin stared right at Eddie with no emotion. When he turned to Rex, his face tightened a fraction; new lines appeared which aged him a good ten years. Rex smiled back, pleased with himself.

"Well, well, well. Rex Milton and Edward Miles." Griffin turned back to Eddie and revealed the tiniest grin.

Eddie thought the office heating broke as he instantly felt several degrees hotter.

"I've waited for this day a long time," Griffin said.

Rex smiled and nodded. "As have we, Chief."

Griffin narrowed his eyes. "Don't call me Chief."

"Sorry, Chief."

"You two picked the wrong day to go AWOL."

Griffin considered himself a gentle soul, but Rex would wind him up. Since the chief of police in action movies was always shouting, Rex thought his boss being angry was part of his charm.

Eddie sensed the impending doom and had to interject, at most he could save himself. "I think Rex and I should be treated separately on this matter—"

"Don't be so modest Eddie." Rex brimmed with pride as if he expected a medal. "We both deserve what we've got coming to us. Right, Chief?"

"This is well overdue, gentlemen. You're both finished."

"Great meeting, Chief." Rex stood.

"He doesn't mean the meeting," Eddie said.

Rex settled back down with a puzzled expression.

"You two are a pair of—"

"Mavericks?" Rex said.

"You both knocked over a fragile old lady."

Rex threw his hands up in the air. "Uh, apprehended a suspect with many stolen items in her bag."

"She had receipts for everything."

"It's a good alibi, I'll give her that. Why didn't she use shopping bags? Huh? Huh?" Rex nodded at Eddie, happy with his victory.

"I think we've lost sight of how separate Rex and I are here. I've only known him since, uh, play school." Eddie buried his head in his hands; he knew he hadn't helped himself with that one.

"Chief, we protect the innocent customer, that's our job. Sure, we use unconventional methods—"

"*He* uses unconventional methods," Eddie said.

"Sure, we harmed and harassed such a customer—"

"*He* harmed and harassed such a customer."

As each of them spoke, Griffin's head turned back and forth.

Rex shook his head. "But don't blame the method."

Eddie nodded. "Blame the method."

"The method works, and if you don't like it, you best take our badges."

"His badge, *his* badge."

Rex struggled to take his plastic name badge off as Eddie sat in shock.

"Both of you. Badges. My desk. Now!"

The pair fidgeted with their IDs as Griffin's eyes burned through their battered skulls. Eddie managed to unpin his and slowly slid it along the desk towards Griffin. Rex fiddled and pulled at his badge.

"Mine won't come off."

Rex and Eddie sat by the window of a dark, dank pub. Shell-shocked, Eddie stared into his pint.

"Come on Eddie, it's not that bad."

"We've been fired from every job we've ever had. We have zero life skills. I can't even join the army."

"Have you tried lately?"

"Not after last time."

"That was because of the chronic sinus infection, right? That's not flared up in ages. You're fine."

"It was the perforated eardrum, which was your fault."

"How was it my fault?"

"Because you jumped down the flume at Waves Leisure Pool before I'd finished. I landed in the pool, and before I got clear of the chute, you flew right out the tube and kicked me in the ear."

"That wasn't my fault. There should have been a life-guard on duty."

"We *were* the lifeguards. Up until that moment anyway." Eddie swished the last of his beer. "I applied again last year, but I was a pound underweight. So I went and ate four quarter pounders for lunch, and when I returned, I puked all over the weighing scales."

Rex laughed enough to choke on his drink. "Are you serious?"

Eddie smiled. "Yeah."

"What did they say?"

"The enrollment office took me to the side and unofficially told me I was too delicate."

Rex winced. "I'm sorry, mate."

"Last time I tried to join the police force, my asthma flared up during the physical. My mum says I always seem to get sick before a big day. She said I sabotage myself."

"That's harsh."

"I asked my doctor if such a condition exists, and he said it's called 'lying'."

"Maybe it's just normal hypochondria?" Rex said.

"I asked about that. The doctor said 'nope, lying'."

"I'll get the beers in, shall I?"

Rex headed to the bar while Eddie mulled over his situation. His only achievement was a 2.2 Bachelor of Arts. Eddie didn't even know what a 2.2 was until after he graduated. While his classmates took photos and ate strawberries with cream, Eddie asked his lecturer to explain what a 2.2 meant. The lecturer told him it meant he was average.

It's kind of an achievement, Eddie thought. *Having a certificate to tell everyone you're a certified average person.*

While Eddie sulked, Rex stood at the bar amazed by a local drunk's magic tricks. Eddie knew Rex didn't give unemployment a single thought. He had a simplicity about him, like how he was adamant the moon is flat, and anyone that said otherwise had been fooled by the government.

Eddie tried not to worry about work. He took a deep breath in and out. Once he managed to calm himself down, Eddie looked out the window and spotted two old homeless men sat at a bus stop.

Oh God, Eddie thought. *That's us. We're gonna be homeless bums.*

Rex plonked a fresh pint in front of Eddie. "Do you think we should've asked the chief for a reference before we left?"

Eddie rolled his eyes and looked over at the homeless pair. One of them peed into the rubbish bin.

"What am I gonna do now? No one's gonna hire us."

Rex grinned. "That's not true. There are still two people that would hire us."

"Who's that?"

Rex's eyes flashed with delight. Eddie was excited for a second, thinking Rex had a genuine trick up his sleeve, but then he realised Rex meant themselves. They were the only two people that would hire them.

"No." Eddie stood up and backed away.

"Come on, you know it makes sense."

"And I suppose you know what type of business we should run?"

"I do, and I think you know what it is as well, if you use your," Rex paused for dramatic effect, "powers of deduction."

"I'm not gonna open a detective agency with you, Rex."

"Why not?"

"I need a real job, one where I can make a real living, make something of myself."

"A boring job, you mean? One with no risks?"

"That's not fair."

"Come on, you don't need Melinda anyway. Girls will fall at our feet when we're detectives. Dangerous, sexy girls. Femme fatales—"

"No."

"You can rub it in Melinda's face."

"Why do you want to work with me?" Eddie said.

"Because, you have a journalism degree, you have a driving licence, we do everything together."

"And why would I want to work with you?"

"Because, we do everything together. We just covered this."

"I don't know, Rex. I need a proper income."

Rex handed Eddie a cut-out from a detective agency's newspaper ad. "Look at the hourly rate, forty quid."

They both earned eight pounds an hour as security guards. Tempted, Eddie ignored all the practical problems and thought about proving himself to Melinda.

He hesitated. "Okay, I'm in."

Rex jumped to his feet and offered his arms. "How about a hug?"

"I'm not really a hugger, Rex."

"I thought you were just saving it for a special occasion."

"I don't think so."

"Come on, bring it in."

Eddie shook his head with discomfort. Rex offered his hand instead, and they shook on it. Rex and Eddie were in business together.

Before the shake was even over, Rex asked: "How much do you have in savings?"

THREE

"Is this it?" Rex asked.

Eddie checked the address. "Three-six-nine High Street. This is the place."

The two friends made disappointed faces as they stood outside the row of Georgian townhouses. Above the ground floor's line of shops, the tall white window frames seemed to pop out compared to the wall's faint salmon colour.

"It's pink," Rex said.

"I think that's salmon."

"Salmon is code for shamefully pink."

They approached a door between the toy shop and the recruitment agency. The door was old and battered. Its black paint had chipped and peeled revealing the previous yellow colour, which had also cracked revealing a coat of red paint.

Eddie pressed the buzzer.

"Please act professional, Rex. I want to give a good impression to the estate agent."

A tall man in his early thirties, dressed in yoga bottoms

and a deep V-neck t-shirt, opened the door. He had a heart-shaped face, a flat nose, shoulder-length jet-black hair, and a stubbly beard.

"Hello, fellas."

"Hi, Jim Jams," Rex said.

"Oh no, what are you doing here?" Eddie asked.

Jim Jams gave a toothy grin. "I'm here to show you around."

"What? You're an estate agent slash drug dealer now?"

"I'm not a drug dealer."

"Sorry, estate agent slash druggie."

"The correct term is bio-hacker, but I don't care to label myself."

Eddie scoffed at the idea.

"It works," Rex said. "Jim Jams developed a regime that means he hasn't had a hangover in five years."

Eddie raised an eyebrow. "Oh really?"

Jim Jams smiled. "It's true. Thanks to a ridiculous combination of booze and narcotics mixed with strategised yoga, green smoothies, supplements, power naps, and the occasional chocolate bar, I'm an optimally functioning human being; which includes not having a hangover for five years."

Eddie gave a dirty look. "Because you haven't been sober in five years, that's why."

"You want to see this place or what?"

The stairs were so narrow, the three of them went up in single file. Halfway down the corridor Rex and Eddie found their new address: Number 4, 369 High Street, Cloisterham, Kent.

Inside, featured a small reception followed by an office space with tall windows and brand new carpet. An old desk sat awkwardly in the centre, and a few dented filing cabinets leaned against a wall. In the corner, a mini-fridge, a microwave, and an electric hob with kettle were stacked on top of each other.

Jim Jams waved his finger around the office. "The previous tenant left the furnishings, and that's a brand new carpet."

Eddie ran his hand along the filing cabinets. A thick layer of dust clung to his fingers.

Rex span around in admiration. "It's perfect."

"Why's it so cheap?" Eddie asked.

"It's been empty for six months," Jim Jams said. "They want it occupied."

"Come on, there has to be something dodgy, or you wouldn't be involved."

"I'm not involved. They just had me install the carpet is all. I told them I knew someone who needed an office."

Rex pointed out the window "Look at that river view. It's lovely."

"You mean the factory silos on the other side of the murky brown water?"

Rex smiled. "I told you it was great."

"How much is it?"

"It's two-hundred-and-fifty a month," Jim Jams said. "Plus one month as deposit, and the first six months in advance."

"Is that normal?" Eddie said.

"You got no credit history, so they're going by my word."

"Are they though? If they take six months rent, are they taking your word or just my money?"

Jim Jams shrugged."Well, my words not worth much."

Eddie did the maths in his head. "So that's one thousand, seven hundred, and fifty pounds.'

"Don't forget the first week's free, and you can keep the furnishings. It's a pucker deal."

"What a steal. Right, Eddie?"

"So what's the catch?"

Jim Jams put his arms around Rex and Eddie. "Can't you be entitled to a lucky day once in a while?"

"A detective needs a car," Rex said.

"I still think we need to wait for our first case. Eight hundred is a lot of money."

The pair swayed in their seats as the bus came to a sudden stop and let a trio of teenagers on. Their mobile phones played hip-hop to the whole bus.

Eddie rolled his eyes. "At least if we had a car we wouldn't have to put up with the likes of DJ Tinny over there."

"That's the spirit."

"But I'm not gonna spend more than eight hundred."

Rex nodded. "Fine."

"I mean it. After paying for the office rent, I've got two thousand, eight hundred and seventy-two pounds in the bank. You've got three-hundred and thirty-nine from—"

"From under my bed."

"And you're sure that's all your savings?"

"I told my nan we started a business and she gave us ten pounds too."

"All the same, our total budget is four-thousand nine-hundred and seventy-one pounds. We have to keep things tight."

"This is our stop."

The pair exited the bus and walked a few doors down. There on the driveway stood the 1971 Morris Minor 1000 Traveller. Rex found the car online for eight hundred pounds and immediately fell in love with it.

Described as an economy car in the same way as a cramped house is called modest, the Morris Minor was a lime-green estate with the passenger section made out of a wooden-frame. The minimal dashboard meant lots of room in the glove compartment for their surveillance gear. It was by no means an antique, but the car was old enough to be considered historic, so Rex and Eddie didn't have to pay road tax.

"What's road tax now?" Rex said. "One hundred and fifty a year? In six years it will have paid for itself."

"If it doesn't fall apart by then," Eddie said.

Scratches, a smashed-in rear light, and leather seats held together with electrical tape showed how much of a mess the car was in. The paint job had faded so much it had a ghostly quality like it haunted the driveway. Although the advert said it only had two previous owners, it failed to mention the current owner was a seventeen-year-old chav. The youthful mouth-breather, decked out in imitation designer sports clothes, swaggered down the driveway with a sneer. Gold bling jangled on his thin frame as he walked.

Although the first owner was a sweet old lady who took good care of the car, the current owner, Tim, managed to clock up an extra sixty thousand miles in little more than nine months.

Eddie bobbed his head side-to-side. "Eight-hundred is a lot of money."

Rex sat in the driver's seat and played with the steering wheel. "It probably cost that much when it was new. That's zero depreciation. It's an investment."

Eddie opened the glove compartment and checked the legal stuff. He was pleased to see the car had just passed the MOT. Now he knew it was road-worthy, or as worthy as a car partly made of wood could be, he was interested.

"Okay, I'll get it as long as we can haggle him down to seven-fifty at most."

Rex smiled. "Thanks, Eddie."

They approached Tim who waxed his new car, a bright red 1999 BMW 3 Series, while the car radio blasted out drum and bass. Tim got the Morris Minor because his parents wanted him to prove he could be trusted with a cheap first car before they bought him something better. When Tim won five thousand pounds on a scratch card and spent it on the new wheels, his life lesson was cut short. He even had enough change to tint the windows and install a DVD player. This was of no interest to Eddie, but he learnt it all the same because Rex kept asking questions.

"What a beauty, and the DVD player is well sweet." Rex forced in chav lingo in the hope of being accepted, or at least not beaten up. "We should get one of these next, Eddie."

"We need to be a bit more inconspicuous than that."

"You sayin' I've got a gay car?" Tim asked, chest puffed out.

"No, I'm not," Eddie said.

How had this escalated so fast? he wondered.

"What you sayin' then?" Tim stepped forward, his pointy face leaned into Eddie's personal space. This would be why Rex talked chav, so he didn't cause offence and accidentally start a fight.

"I mean we don't want to get noticed, that's all." Eddie realised how ridiculous this sounded when he remembered he was buying a lime-green car with wooden framing. "The BMW is great, it's masculine, it's bold, it's, uh, it's—"

"He's saying you have a wicked ride," Rex chimed in. "Everyone is gonna notice how cool it is."

Tim relaxed. "Thanks, mate."

"Will you take seven-hundred for it?" Eddie asked.

Tim licked his teeth. "Go on then."

Rex raised a finger for attention. "What about seven-fifty?"

"Sold."

"Rex, what are you doing?"

"Haggling?"

"Up?"

"Oh, right, sorry about that."

Eddie pursed his lips. "I'll get the seven-hundred."

"Sorry, mate. But this fella's giving me seven hundred and fifty."

"What? No, he's not," Eddie said. "Tell him you're not."

"I'm not."

Tim thumped Rex in the shoulder. "You gotta stand up for yourself mate, don't back down like that. He's trying to steal the car from right under yah."

Misinterpreting the playful push as physical violence, Rex didn't know what to do. "Yeah, okay. Seven-fifty it is."

"That's more like it."

"Fine," Eddie snapped, knowing he was on the losing end of an idiotic argument. "Seven-fifty." He counted the money and passed it to Tim.

"Nah mate, you can't offer the same as the competition's bid," Tim tipped his head towards Rex. "He still gets it."

"We're not separate buyers. Rex and I are together."

"Together, eh?" Tim turned to Rex "This true? Are you and him, together?"

Rex's body froze, only his eyes shifted. Violence always sent him inward. In a panic, he'd forgotten about the car and thought this was a mugging.

"Oi? Don't ignore me. It's disrespectful. Are you two together?"

Rex turned to Eddie and back at Tim.

"No."

Eddie raised his hands. "What are you saying?"

Rex thought he was being asked if they were a couple. Tim's push followed by his irritated tone made Rex believe he was about to become the victim of a misidentified hate-crime.

"Look mate, if you want it, you're gonna have to offer more than my man here."

Eddie sneered. "Fine, seven hundred and fifty-one."

"It's in increments of fifty."

"Oh right, so you don't know what inconspicuous means but you know the word increment?"

Tim's beady eyes stared Eddie down.

"Fine, eight hundred." Eddie pulled out the extra fifty and made the exchange.

Rex and Eddie got in the car. Eddie was the driver since Rex had never taken driving lessons. Tim knocked on the driver's window. Eddie turned the hand crank to lower the glass.

"I just want to say, I know you gay boys get a hard time, but I wish you a lifetime of happiness."

Eddie forced a smile. "Thanks, but we're business partners." Tim cocked his head in confusion. "Tell him, Rex."

Rex sat in his seat, hands on his thighs, head hung low. He still hadn't gotten over his fright.

"All right mate, I get yah." Tim gave a wink and patted the car as he left.

Eddie insisted they repaint the office's grubby walls. The clean new carpet highlighted the wall's marks, stains and general nastiness. They laid newspaper down close to the walls and applied primer.

"Rex, will you open the window?" Eddie asked. "The paint fumes have gone to my head."

Rex worked his way over to the window and gave it a yank. It didn't budge. He felt cheated and pulled harder.

"Push it up."

"I did push it up. It's jammed."

Eddie joined him. They both tugged the window at the same time. It would not move.

"It's useless," Rex said.

"Try harder."

Rex gave the handle a massive pull, and it snapped off. He stumbled backwards and tripped as he knocked over the paint can, which dumped the paint onto the carpet.

"No, no, no," Eddie yelled as he jumped over Rex and grabbed the can. It was already half empty. The thick white primer consumed the carpet as it stretched out.

"I'm fine thanks," Rex grumbled as he pulled himself back up.

Eddie tried to push the puddle of paint back into the can."Do you know what this means?"

"We've lost our deposit?"

"My deposit. And they can kick us out. Which means they'd keep all six months of the rent."

"It's not too bad. We just need a bit of paint thinner."

"And have a four-foot wide stain?"

"Okay, so if we paint the whole floor then use the paint thinner, it will all match."

Eddie huffed. "We have to take up the carpet and deny we ever had any. That'll work. Right?"

Rex raided the maintenance cupboard for a Stanley knife and ripped up the carpet piece-by-piece. Once the black bin bag was full Eddie snuck it out and dumped the contents in the building's wheelie bin. When Eddie returned to the office, he found Rex sat on the desk.

"What are you doing?" Eddie asked.

"Nothing?"

"Is that a question?"

Rex crossed his arms and legs. "No?"

"You said that as a question as well."

"Did I?"

"You need help moving the desk?"

"I like it here."

"We need to get the carpet from underneath it."

"What if, we cut around it and left some carpet under the desk? Like a rug. There's hardly any paint on this part."

"Just lift the other end of the table."

Rex jumped off and grabbed the desk's end. Eddie lifted his side, but Rex struggled to raise his.

"Lift, Rex."

"I am lifting," he said with mock strain. He made a big dramatic sigh like he'd given up. "I think my end is broken."

"Lift with your back," Eddie said in a strained voice.

"I lift with my hands."

"Yes, hold it with your hands, but support it with your back."

Rex shook his head like he'd been asked to do the impossible. Something wasn't right.

Eddie placed his hands on his hips. "What are you hiding?"

"Nothing."

Eddie slid his table end onto the wood floor and lifted the carpet. Underneath, he found a faded chalk outline in the shape of a man slumped on the floor with a red cloud of tiny dots spread around the head.

FOUR

"Rex, did you know about this?"

"I just saw it while you took out the carpet."

Eddie knelt by the chalk outline. "You knew someone died here, didn't you?"

"I'm sure it cleans off easily."

"Really? Because the red stains have been heavily brushed."

Rex shrugged. "Wood *is* porous."

Eddie paced up and down the room. "Bloody Jim Jams. You knew about this, didn't you?"

"You said you wanted a cheap office."

"Tell me they caught the killer?"

"Yes ... Maybe... I don't know. The Door Knock Killer did it. Has he been caught?"

"Oh, please."

"It's true. He knocks three times before entering and kills everyone that heard."

"If he killed everyone that heard, how does anyone know about it?"

KNOCK, KNOCK, KNOCK. The rattling door made them both jump.

"Uh, get the door, Rex."

"You're closer."

Eddie took two deliberate steps away from the door. The handle rattled and turned. The door opened and in stepped Harold the cleaner.

"Have you got a woodie?" he asked.

Eddie cocked his head. "I beg your pardon?"

"A woodie. Do either of you have a woodie?"

"No."

Harold hurried off and slammed the door shut.

Eddie turned to Rex. "What was that about?"

Rex shrugged. "Man's looking for a woodie."

Outside the hallway, Harold shouted: "Does anyone here have a woodie? Anyone?"

Rex and Eddie popped their heads out the door, as did those from the other offices in the corridor.

"I'm looking for the owner of a woodie," he called out. "A lime green woodie."

Oh crap, Eddie thought. He realised Harold meant the Morris Minor.

"Me!" Eddie said. "I've got a woodie." The other occupants all stared at him. "I mean, a Morris Minor."

"It's getting towed."

Eddie ran outside in enough time to watch the tow truck drive off with their car. He'd forgotten there was no parking after four o'clock to allow a second lane during rush hour.

Knowing at least another hundred quid just drove down the street, Eddie sighed in defeat and walked back to his office of death. Inside he saw Rex trying to remove the chalk outline with damp toilet roll.

Eddie slumped on the desk. "So, you knew about the

killing."

"You said you wanted a cheap office."

"Now they've got six months rent, so we're stuck here. Perfect."

"Calm down Eddie, they caught the killer, I think."

"I'm googling it."

Within fifteen minutes, Eddie found news stories of the death of a sixty-eight-year-old man named Derek Lawrence. He was an ex-TV writer who used the office to write novels, none of them published. The man led a quiet life upsetting no one. It was not believed to be the Door Knock Killer, as he always removed the bodies. Many theorised the victim had been mistaken for someone else and wrongfully assassinated.

"The murder wasn't solved," Eddie said. "The killer wore gloves, so there were no fingerprints. He entered, shot him in the back of the head, and left. That's horrible."

"It's a bit boring if you ask me," Rex said. "At least the Door Knock Killer has a gimmick."

Eddie furrowed his brow. "So you're not upset about the brutality, you're just annoyed it's a plain old-fashioned murder? That it's not creative enough for you?"

Rex bobbed his head. "Yeah."

"I think if they were more creative, they'd find better solutions to their problems than killing people."

"You're right. Who am I to judge? I suppose he's efficient at least. There is a quiet confidence to not overthinking these things."

Eddie stared at the dried bloodstains a little too long. "Why didn't the building pay extra to re-sand the floor?"

"I don't know, maybe the brains spread out a little more than they expected. If you think about it, they did a pretty good cleaning job."

"They used bleach, right?" Eddie's heart rate

increased. "I mean, it's not like we've got microscopic brain cells in our fingernails or anything." He bent over in a fit of anxiety and dizziness.

"Eddie, you're freaking out. At worst it was a case of mistaken identity. That must make you feel a little safer."

"That means it was a random killing. How are we safer? Anytime, anywhere, a killer may kill you for no reason. Does that sound safe to you? Does it?"

Lightheaded and out of breath, Eddie used the desk as support and lowered himself to the floor. Rex pulled a brown paper bag out of his blazer pocket, emptied out the leftover sweet wrappers and handed Eddie the bag.

"Breathe into this."

Eddie took a deep breath in and sucked up a loose boiled sweet Rex accidentally left in the bag. Eddie choked. With the sweet lodged at the back of his throat, the anxiety didn't seem so bad after all.

"Are you okay?" Rex asked.

Eddie turned a shade of bright red. He tried to lift himself up, but his hand slid across the wall thanks to the still wet paint. Without anything to grip, Eddie skidded across the wet wall until his back smeared along the paint. Rex peeled Eddie off the wall and slapped his back as hard as he could. Still choking, Eddie's face turned from red to purple.

"Hold on."

Rex wiped his paint-covered hand on Eddie's already ruined shirt and gently took off his own blazer. He folded it, put it on the desk, and gave Eddie the Heimlich manoeuvre. After a few violent squeezes, the sweet dislodged and flung across the floor.

"Are you okay?"

Eddie pushed Rex away, whose front was now covered in paint from Eddie's back.

"I'm insane. Absolutely insane," Eddie declared.

"I'm sorry."

"No, it's my fault. I said yes, to that car, to the office, to investing nearly every penny I own into a foolhardy detective business."

Rex hung his head.

"Every job we've ever had we've been fired from, so I'm gonna shorten my misery and fire myself."

Eddie stormed out the office with his car keys in hand. He entered the street and remembered the car was gone. After a little strop, he walked towards home.

Rex chased after him. "I'm sorry, Eddie."

"I'm not talking to you after what you've done to me."

A young mother pushing a pram passed them on the street. She gazed at the paint all down Eddie's back and the paint covering Rex's front.

Eddie shook his arms. "Not that. We weren't doing that. We're just friends."

She picked up her pace as new pedestrians gawked at the pair.

"We're still friends then?" Rex said, hopeful.

A group of chav teens pointed, laughed, and called them "Bummers."

"A picture will last longer," Eddie said.

The teens pulled their camera phones out and snapped away.

"It's a figure of speech." Eddie threw his arms in defeat and turned to Rex, who posed for the photos with a broad smile. Eddie shook his head and marched home.

The next morning, Eddie woke up clear-headed. He put on a suit and went back to The Octagon Shopping Centre.

Without Rex there he decided he had at least half a chance of getting Griffin to rehire him.

Griffin placed tweezers in his half-built ship in a bottle. "Can't do anything for you."

"Please, you've got to save me."

"I sympathise Edward, but if I re-hire you, I'll have to re-hire Rex."

Eddie shifted forward in the chair. "No, no you won't, it'll be our secret."

"Too risky. I don't want that crackpot here as a customer, let alone as an employee."

"Come on, he's not that bad. He's a good friend, and he's been a passionate business partner."

Griffin smirked. "Business partner?"

Eddie dropped to his knees. "I know, I made a mistake. Please don't send me back to him. I want my job back."

The door knocked, and Rex entered with a bouquet of flowers.

"Hey Chief, just popped by to—" Rex noticed Eddie kneeling on the floor. Filled with embarrassment, Eddie jumped back on his feet. They both felt caught with their figurative trousers down.

"What are you doing here?" Eddie asked.

Rex smiled wide. "Visiting?"

"You're trying to get your job back, aren't you?"

"No."

Griffin folded his arms. "I told you yesterday, Rex. I ain't hiring."

"You were here yesterday as well?"

Rex chortled. "Chief's joking." He placed the flowers next to an identical, day-old, bouquet. "You know the chief and his crazy sense of humour."

Eddie placed his hands on his hips. "So why are you here?"

"I came for … my lamp." He grabbed a random lamp off the filing cabinet.

"Put the lamp down, Rex," Griffin said.

"It's my lamp, Chief."

"Don't call me Chief." Griffin squeezed his tweezers too hard and snapped his ship's mast.

Rex leaned in close to Eddie. "Seriously, you can't lend this man anything."

"That's it. Get out of my office. You two harass me again, and I'll ban you both from the whole damn shopping centre."

"Over a lamp?" Rex asked.

"Get out!" Griffin jumped from his seat in a rage and pounded both hands on his desk, which knocked his ship in a bottle. It rolled off the table and shattered into smithereens.

"Rex, I believe our ship has sailed."

"One. More. Word," Griffin growled. "I dare you."

Eddie sped towards the door and dragged Rex along with him. Rex lifted his hand to his ear like a phone and mouthed, "Call me."

Griffin threw a second ship in a bottle at the door as Eddie closed it.

"He'll call," Rex said. "So, what do you want to do today?"

"Now my last chance of getting my job back went from never to never ever? Well, I think I shall go home, curl up into the foetal position, and cry until I'm resigned to the fact no one will ever hire me."

"But someone wants to hire us."

Eddie's eyes widened. "A client called?"

Rex bobbed his head. "Sort of."

"Goodbye, Rex."

"No listen, there's a reward for information on the murderer of the old man in our office."

Eddie waved his hands dismissively and walked down the corridor.

"Five grand," Rex said.

Eddie stopped. "Five grand? For what?"

"Information proving who the killer is. His daughter is offering five thousand quid for it."

"It's tempting, but I think the whole detective thing was a mistake. We should quit while we still have some money left. Find another job."

"As what? Security guards, lifeguards, that summer we were paperboys."

"We were kids back then."

"No, the second time, three summers ago."

Eddie's shoulders slumped. "Oh, right. I think I forgot that on purpose."

"There aren't any good jobs for us."

"It's too risky. I've practically lost everything I saved."

Rex gave a gentle smile. "But not quite everything."

"Is that meant to be a silver lining or something?"

"Think of it this way, if we find the killer, you get the five grand, I get the credit. You'll get your investment back plus change, I get the fame and glory, and we both go our separate ways."

"Why not separate now?"

"It's my first case, Eddie. I can't do it without you. We do everything together."

Eddie sighed. "But we split after the case?"

"I promise."

"Done." Eddie offered out his hand, and they shook on it.

Rex smiled. "Or at the most until I get my own driving licence."

FIVE

Eddie passed over the ticket and leaned on the impound office's counter. "I'm here to pay a fine."

The gruff-looking man took the ticket and glared at Eddie. "What's that in your hair?"

Eddie grabbed the hair behind his ear and felt the dried paint from yesterday. "None of your business."

Rex gazed in wonder at the decor: hubcaps, licence plates and other car parts hung from the wall. Rex enjoyed it all except the nude calendar, which he completely overlooked.

"You the owner?" the gruff man asked.

Eddie narrowed his eyes. "Yes."

"Cash or credit."

"Cash."

The gruff man picked up his radio. "Phil, the man with the woodie is here."

Rex sniggered.

"Why do people keep calling it that? It's a Morris Minor."

"That's what people call it," the gruff man said.

"What people?"

"Dunno, people that don't own a car made of wood."

Rex laughed. "Nice one mate."

"Rex, did you know it was called a woodie?"

"My nan called it that when I showed her the ad. But she can't tell the difference between the remote control and the wireless phone, so I didn't take her too seriously."

"We see a lot of cars come through here, not many wood— uh, Morris Minors anymore. They say the wooden frame was phased out for more sturdy, reliable, material."

"Yes, thanks for that. May I have my car now?"

The man typed into the mechanical cash register. "That will be one hundred and twenty pounds."

The Morris Minor spluttered and puffed along the winding country path towards a large cottage in Snodling village. The village was north of the River Invicta about twenty minutes west of Cloisterham. Rex and Eddie thought the house was posh, but in Cloisterham, anywhere out in the countryside was considered posh.

Rex jumped out of the car and practically skipped to the big red front door. He tapped a jaunty tune with the brass doorknocker.

"Please calm down," Eddie begged.

"Do you think she'll be our first femme fatale?"

"I think she's a grieving woman."

"Right, so, innocent victim. She'll need a shoulder to cry on."

Eddie grimaced. "Don't be creepy."

Rex crossed his arms over his chest. "How's that creepy?"

"She needs information on her father's murder. We will show her understanding and compassion."

"How's that different from what I said?"

The door opened and Stacey Lawrence, early thirties with bleach-blonde hair, opened the door. Heavy black eyeshadow highlighted her milky complexion. Rex thought her make-up made her smoulder, Eddie thought she looked like a panda, but a sexy panda all the same. Eddie noticed her simple yellow dress was covered in creases, like she'd just thrown it on.

"You're the detectives?"

"Um, yes," Eddie said.

"You better come in."

The house was a traditional white cottage with a thatched roof. The walls were painted pastel colours and dark antique furniture spread across each room. Although the cottage had large windows, the thick red drapes were pulled and let only a sliver of light into each room.

Stacey guided them to the kitchen. She stood at the kitchen island while the pair propped themselves on the high stools.

"Thanks for seeing us," Eddie said.

She grabbed a bottle of vodka, poured a generous shot, and nodded her head to a display of spirits. "Would either of you like a drink?"

Eddie raised his palms. "I'm fine thanks."

"Me too."

"Come on, someone's got to drink with me."

"Cup of tea would be lovely," Rex said.

She took a moment to work out if Rex was serious.

"Is he for real?"

Eddie gave a subtle nod. "I'm afraid so."

She turned to Rex. "You want a cup of tea?"

"Yes, please. No milk, two sugars, and a lemon slice if you have it?"

"Because I've got spirits."

"I won't trouble you with that. Just a tea for me, thanks."

"And you?"

Eddie wasn't sure what to say. It seemed rude to say no, but it didn't look like she wanted to make one either. "If you're making one."

Stacey rolled her eyes and filled the kettle. She put the kettle on the hot stove and searched the cupboards for tea bags. She seemed frazzled and unsure of herself. "Sorry, I'm a little hungover."

Eddie gave a polite smile. "No worries."

Stacey checked inside a clay pot and found the tea bags. "There we are." She dropped them into two mugs.

"So, what did you find out?"

"Pardon?" Eddie asked.

"You have information on my father's death, right?"

"Not exactly," Eddie said. He turned to Rex who had lowered his head like a dog caught on the sofa.

"You don't have information on my father then?"

"We know he was murdered," Rex said. "And that he died in our office on October twenty-eighth, and that his blood was very hard to clean—"

"What he means is, uh, we know the basic details."

"You want a reward for telling me what I already know?" Her eyebrows furrowed as her eyes glazed over with the threat of tears. Embarrassed, Eddie avoided eye contact. Rex scratched his head. The kettle's whistle broke the awkward silence.

"We're detectives," Rex said. "We think we can solve your case and wanted to know a bit more about your father."

"I'm confused, are you here for the reward?"

"Yes," Rex said.

"There seems to have been a bit of a mix-up," Eddie said. "We were here to take the case so we can bring you information, you know, later. But it seems what you want is to give a reward to someone that already knows."

She stirred the tea and pushed the cups towards them, along with a pot of sugar and a pint of milk.

"So I offer a five grand reward for information, and you come to me looking for a lead?"

Eddie felt sick to his stomach. He'd come into a woman's home and brought up her family tragedy with nothing to offer.

"Actually," Rex said. "It's standard detective practice to get half now, half later—"

"Rex, stop it."

"Or at least set up a retainer for expenses."

"Shut up, Rex."

She downed her vodka and laughed. Rex didn't get what was funny but realised he'd lost her interest. "The full amount after would work too."

"You gonna drink your tea?" she said.

Eddie obediently sipped away, but Rex raised a hand.

"I actually asked for a slice of lemon."

"I don't have any lemons."

Rex pointed across the room at a fruit bowl with a few lemons in it.

"You want a lemon?"

"Yes, please."

"I'll give you a lemon." Stacey threw the yellow fruit at Rex, and it bounced off his head, which Rex didn't seem to mind at all. She picked up the lemons and threw them at Rex and Eddie. Eddie jumped out of his seat. He spilt tea on his hand and still took a lemon to the gut. The pure force winded him a little.

"Get the hell out of my house."

"Come on, Rex, we're leaving."

Rex froze again. Eddie grabbed his hand and marched out of the house as Stacey threw oranges, apples and then a mango. Her ammunition got bigger and bigger. Eddie saw she owned a pineapple and wanted to get in the car before she threw that too.

"I don't like that lady very much," Rex said, breaking a ten-minute silence as they drove through the countryside. "I mean, why offer a cup of tea and then get all upset like that?"

Eddie clenched the steering wheel. "She was upset because she thought we had information on her father's murderer. She wasn't looking to hire two detectives without any clue on the murder at all."

Rex stared at Eddie, blank-faced. He giggled. "That's embarrassing."

"I think its best we head to the office. I'll collect my things, and we can just call it even."

"What? You can't do that. You said you'd help me with my first case."

"Because I thought you *had* a case."

"I'll get another one, and you'll get your investment back."

"I'll get some money when I sell the car." Eddie was interrupted by a nasty clunk from hitting a pothole. Within another mile, they had a flat tyre.

The rest of their afternoon consisted of fixing the car. After learning they didn't have a spare wheel, they rolled the tyre into town. The mechanic told them the extra mile tore through the rubber, so they'd need a new one. Rex and Eddie didn't speak to each other the entire trip. Rex helped Eddie carry and install the new tyre in perfect silence. It's what Eddie needed.

At the office, Eddie packed his things. Rex walked up to the answer machine and pushed a button next to a flashing light.

"Hi, this is Stacey Lawrence. I'm calling to apologise about earlier. I've been having a rough time at the moment. If you find out who killed my father, I would, of course, pay you the reward. And, yeah, sorry about the fruiting. Thanks, bye."

Rex's face lit up. "What do you say, Eddie?"

Eddie took a deep breath. He thought about his savings and how he desperately wanted the money back. Rex's smile cracked, and Eddie saw the desperation in his eyes.

"Fine. Let's give it a go."

Eddie sat at the computer with Rex over his shoulder and searched for Derek Lawrence. The Kent Gazette website featured an obituary on the victim.

Rex leaned closer. "What does it say?"

"It says Derek Lawrence passed away at his personal office."

"That's putting it mildly."

Eddie scrolled through the article. "He was a successful writer in the late seventies, but didn't do much after that. Lawrence started out as a journalist for The Cloisterham Daily, writing about his time riding along with the police."

"Cool, I've always wanted to ride in a police car."

"In nineteen sixty-nine he published Taskforce, a book about his experiences with the local police. In nineteen seventy-two the BBC produced a Taskforce TV show which ran for ten years. The show was even filmed in Cloisterham."

"Nan likes that show. They used to repeat it weekday afternoons," Rex said.

"After the show was cancelled, he continued to write, but he struggled to find a publisher." Eddie sighed. "Well, this isn't much good. We've got nothing from nineteen eighty-three onwards."

Rex stood up straight. "I could ask around. See what the neighbours say."

While Rex was out, Eddie scrolled through web page after web page but learnt nothing new about Lawrence.

Rex entered the office with his lower lip slightly puffed out.

Eddie peered over the monitor. "No luck?"

"No one even knew his name. He's been here since the eighties and never talked to anyone. What did the Internet say?"

"Taskforce has a message board, but it's mostly fan theories, like what the characters would be up to now."

"Did you ask them for help?"

Eddie frowned. "I can't. After I pointed out most of the characters would be dead by now, they blocked my account."

"Let me try."

Rex created an account and searched the message board.

"Check this out. It's behind-the-scenes photos of filming."

Eddie leaned in and examined the pictures. It showed a jolly middle-aged Lawrence with his feet up on a desk. Other shots showed cameras and clapperboards in front of actors with puffy hairstyles. One outdoor photo showed the TV studio in the background.

Eddie leaned in closer. “I know that building.”

“It’s Laser Flux. The laser tag place.” Rex bounced up and down as he spoke.

“That’s still open? I haven’t been there in ten years.”

“I bet it’s still awesome.”

Eddie searched the message board for the TV studio and found a post from an ex-employee of Laser Flux. Although the studio became a futuristic battlefield for teens to play out their violent fantasies, the upstairs production office was untouched.

“Evidence! Can we go to Laser Flux, Eddie? Can we?”

“I don’t think they’re gonna let us in their office.

“Come on.”

“But it’s the only lead we have,” Eddie said. “We’ll have to go undercover.”

SIX

Eddie's heart beat a little faster as he and Rex entered the Laser Flux reception. His eyes adjusted to the lack of light in the dark reception room. The walls were covered in silver painted plywood with flashing Christmas lights attached. As a youth, Eddie thought the UV black lights made everything look like a futuristic alien world. Now, he noticed how much it showed up his dandruff. Rex nodded with an expression that said, "It's good to be back."

Eddie scrunched his nose. "They haven't changed a thing."

"Great, isn't it?"

The pair reached a short round lady with a blonde beehive at the cash register.

"That's fifteen-pound total?" Eddie asked.

"Each," she said.

"Thirty quid?"

"That's right."

Rex jumped on the spot as Eddie forked over the money.

"Wait on the blue line with your team members. When the red lights flash, you have one minute to put on your gear and fifteen minutes in the arena."

Rex and Eddie lined up with two fourteen-year-old boys and a twelve-year-old girl. The young teens looked them up and down with disgust.

The girl stepped forward. "How old are you?"

"Twenty-eight," Eddie said.

"That's well old."

Rex smiled. "We're seasoned professionals. We've got your back."

"Wouldn't you rather go on the next round?" the skinny boy asked. "That way you'd get to play with your carer?"

Eddie narrowed his eyes. "My what?"

"Whoever takes care of you," the girl said.

The chubby boy laughed. "You really ain't with it, are you? Man, I can't believe we got stuck with the special bus."

The skinny boy nodded in agreement.

Rex crossed his arms. "You think we're retarded?"

All three nodded.

Eddie wagged his finger. "That is both politically, and factually, incorrect."

"Then why are you adults playing a game for people our age?" the girl asked.

Eddie crouched over them. "Adults can play laser tag."

The chubby boy shook his head. "Real adults do paintball. They probably don't let you 'cause you'll eat the paint."

The girl cocked her head. "Where's the rest of them? I thought you only travel by the busload."

"We didn't come here in a bus," Eddie said.

"What did you come in then?"

Eddie hesitated. "I don't want to talk about it."

The skinny boy inspected the reception. "Does your carer even know you are here?"

Eddie pointed at Rex. "How do you know I'm not his carer?"

All three teens raised an eyebrow.

"What's that supposed to mean?" Eddie said.

Confused, Rex looked behind him to see who Eddie pointed at.

The girl giggled. "You're a pair of window-lickers."

Eddie put his hands on his hip. "We are an asset to this team."

"Whatever," the girl said.

The three teens dismissed the pair and talked amongst themselves.

Rex tapped Eddie on the shoulder. "Check out the competition, they look mean." Eddie turned to the red team's line and saw a group of small pre-teen boys.

"They're pygmies compared to us. I think we'll be fine. Remember, our goal is to get inside and sneak off to the office. I reckon a fire exit will lead us there."

"But if we score a few points while we're at it, no harm, no foul?"

"We aren't here to play games—"

A siren blared as a red light above the doorway flashed.

"Battle commences in t-minus one minute," a robotic female voice announced. "Put on your body armour and wait at the arena entrance for instructions."

In the weapon's chamber, they put on their blue body armour and laser gun.

At the doorway, the chubby boy turned and faced the rest of the blues. "Okay, team. Head for the shadows and let the enemy come to you. Softly, softly, catchee monkey."

Eddie nudged Rex. "Check out little captain commando."

"You got a problem?" the boy barked.

Startled, Eddie averted his eyes. "Uh, me? No."

"We are in a war," the chubby boy said. "If you can't keep up, then you hide until it's over. You mess this up, and I will pistol whip you in the face." The boy's chubby cheeks jiggled as he shouted.

Eddie tucked his chin in. "All right, calm down."

"I think he's serious, Eddie."

The boy stepped forward. "Can I count on you?"

Eddie didn't want to draw unnecessary attention and swallowed his pride. "Yes, sir."

The arena doors burst open, and smoke blew down.

The chubby captain charged forward. "Go, go, go!"

The teens ran off into the shadows. Rex dropped and rolled into the mist. Eddie was alone.

The arena was lit by neon blues, reds and yellows. UV black lights covered the halls, but there were plenty of dark nooks and crannies. Speakers all around the arena played drum and bass so loud Eddie could feel his skeleton reverberate. A steel stairway led to a second level with a metal grate floor that allowed people to shoot each other from above and below.

"Rex? Rex, where are you?" One of the red pygmies dashed past and shot Eddie. His chest plate rumbled and sent a small electric jolt into his chest. "Ow, that really—"

Zap! Eddie was shot a second time in the back and received another jolt to his spine.

"What the hell?" He tried to shoot back, but his laser gun was stunned from the hit. The little red pygmies disappeared before Eddie's weapon recharged.

Eddie knew his guns would freeze for five-seconds after

taking a hit, but he didn't remember being electrocuted before. He wondered if it was a new feature until he noticed a few exposed wires on his body armour. After fifteen years of daily abuse, the body packs were getting their revenge.

A fire exit sign glowed at the end of a long smoky corridor. Eddie ran towards the door's gleaming push bar. A little red team member jumped out in front of him with a laser gun pointed at Eddie's chest. Zap! The little tyke shuddered. He'd been sniped by Rex, who hid in the shadows.

"Come on, Eddie." Rex waved Eddie over to the fire exit. "I've got you covered."

Eddie speed-walked to the exit as Rex travelled backwards to scan for enemies.

Three red soldiers jumped out and shot Rex. His body pack lit up with flashing LEDs, and the shock knocked him back. Rex crashed into Eddie, which shoved them both into the fire exit door and shared the electric shock. The weight of the pair forced the door open. Rex rolled off a squashed Eddie, who uncontrollably shook from the triple voltage.

"What a buzz, eh Eddie?"

"Are you getting electrocuted too?" Eddie asked.

"Yeah, who knew you could improve laser tag? Ups the stakes, makes you feel alive."

"The game lasts fifteen minutes, so we have maybe twelve minutes at most to check the office before anyone knows we're missing."

Rex followed Eddie up the flight of stairs. On the landing, they came face-to-face with a cleaning lady, a Jamaican woman with a stoic face. Eddie knew he had to come up with a story fast.

"Um, hello." His mind went blank. *Not the best start*, he thought.

"What you want?" she asked.

"Can we check out the old office?" Rex asked, as if it was a reasonable request for two adults in laser tag gear to make.

"No."

"Okay, thanks," Rex headed back down the stairs. Eddie pulled him back.

"Can we come to an arrangement?" Eddie asked. "Ten quid?"

The Cleaner scowled. "Fifty quid."

"Twenty?"

"Fifty."

"Oh, come on, we just want ten minutes. That's all."

"Fifty."

"I can maybe push thirty?"

"No."

"We've got to be back out there soon, I can't spend all my time negotiating with you."

"You call this a negotiation?" she said.

"She has a point, Eddie."

The cleaner tapped her watch. "Nine minutes."

"Fine." Eddie opened up his wallet and pulled out fifty pounds. He took a moment to mentally calculate what he had left. Their cash flow was down to eight hundred and sixty pounds.

Once she found the right key, they had six minutes left. She opened the door, and Rex and Eddie barged through. A mess of yellowed papers, all stacked in piles, laid untouched. They both rummaged through files finding scripts, location reports, and equipment rental receipts. None of it was of any use to them.

"Is this something?" Rex asked.

He rushed over to Eddie carrying a memo addressed to the Head of Drama.

Eddie read: Although it is with great hesitation, I must report Derek Lawrence is no longer fit to run this show. He must submit his resignation before he causes permanent damage to the show and jeopardises the jobs of hundreds of people. Signed John Laing, Co-Executive Producer.

"A grudge? It's a start," Eddie said. With a minute to spare they ran out of the office to the stairwell. In the hallway, a new cleaner, a Polish woman so thin her skin tightly wrapped around her skeleton, stared at the pair.

"Act natural," Eddie whispered to Rex. "Excuse us." They squeezed past her trolley.

"What you do here?" she asked.

"We're just leaving."

"What is paper for?"

"It's nothing."

She folded her arms. "You not to be here."

"We're off now, bye."

"I tell boss."

Eddie cringed. "No, don't tell boss. We've already paid a bribe."

"Bribe, yes. Okay."

Eddie turned to Rex. "She understands. It's all good."

Rex and Eddie headed down the stairs.

The Polish woman cleared her throat. "You pay bribe, then you go."

"No, we, we already paid the bribe," Eddie said

"No."

"To the Jamaican lady," Rex explained.

"We paid her ten minutes ago," Eddie added.

"Her shift over."

"Yes, well, if you speak to her, she can split her bribe with you. Twenty-five pounds."

"Twenty-five. Okay." She held out her hand.

"No, you don't understand, my friend and I have to go. You have to speak to the other cleaner. That's it. Come on, Rex."

They scrambled down a few more steps. The Polish lady lifted her radio and called into it. "Yvonne to Management."

"Fine, twenty-five." Eddie rushed over and opened his wallet. "I don't have any fives, do you have change?"

She didn't do or say anything. It seemed like a tactic, the first one to speak would be the loser.

Why break the habit of a lifetime? Eddie thought.

"Of course, you don't. Here." He handed over thirty quids' worth of hush money. "Let's get out of here before a third cleaner shows up."

The pair rushed down the stairs and burst back into the arena. The scoreboards showed the blues were losing big time: 21-9. With five reds against three blues, it was a massacre. The dodgy electrocuting body packs left the skinny blue teen rolling on the ground in tears. The girl ran by as two reds continually shot her in the back. She couldn't recharge her gun because she took repeated electric jolts.

Rex turned to Eddie. "It's payback time." He dropped and rolled.

"What purpose does that serve?" Eddie said.

"It's cool."

Rex sprinted into the central area, a circular space that all corridors led to. Rex stood over the third blue team-member, the chubby captain, now hunched up in a ball. He could view every corner of the arena, and revealed himself to every player. Rex yodelled a Tarzan-like call and declared, "Come and get me." Out of the dark corridors, the red pygmy army charged at him from every direction.

Rex picked up the blue captain's laser gun and swung around firing down each hall. With two lasers, he zapped each red player in seconds. They continued to run at him as their body packs sent an electric current through their tiny rib cages. Rex was so fast he could shoot each one every five seconds, which kept their weapons stunned. They were so busy taking volts to the heart, they didn't have a chance to run away. With thirty seconds until the battle ended, Rex evened out the scoreboard. The red team fell to their knees and cried as Rex mercilessly fired at them one at a time until the siren sounded. 28-42 to the blues.

Eddie could not think for the sound of crying in the Laser Flux reception. The five little pre-teens, previously in red battle-gear, bawled their little hearts out. The parents tried to console their young, but every time they attempted to hug their little ones, a static shock would zap back. The emotional kids were too upset to explain Rex's repeat executions and pointed at him instead. The adults gave Rex and Eddie shaming looks. The forehead vein of a skinhead father pulsed with intensity as he eyeballed the pair.

Rex nudged Eddie. "What's their problem?"

"I think they just wanted a fun little game."

"Anyone that thinks it's a game doesn't respect laser tag."

As Rex lined up to get his scorecard, Eddie mouthed "sorry" to the parents and kids. Eddie grabbed his scorecard. He'd been hit five times and shot no one. Rex had received three hits and shot people thirty-two times. His scorecard read, *Well Done, Rambo.* Eddie's said, *Put your affairs in order, you're a walking target.*

Back at the office, Rex and Eddie studied the Taskforce message boards for anything related to the memo's author, John Laing.

Rex pointed at the screen. "This says he was a TV writer and producer who worked with Derek Lawrence on the show."

Eddie rolled his eyes. "I managed to work that much out from the memo."

"The message board is split. Some think Laing was the real brains, others think he ruined the show. Both writers always argued and bickered."

Eddie rubbed his chin. "Where is he now?"

"Well, eventually they both got sacked, and they both blamed each other. That's motive."

Eddie bobbed his head, unsatisfied. "We need a bit more than that to go on."

Rex scrolled through several messages and found a quote by Laing.

"Derek Lawrence deserves cancer," he read aloud. "I hope his cancer gets cancer, and he dies twice as fast. They can call it Derek Lawrence disease, it's the only thing that talentless hack deserves to be famous for."

Eddie raised his eyebrows. "Okay, that's a bit like motive."

"He did it," Rex said.

"Come on, he was fired from one job decades ago. I'm sure he's moved on."

"He wrote letters to the BBC to tell them what he thought of them too. He didn't work in TV again after that. Maybe he got bitter when he found out Lawrence was still writing."

"Let's get our hands on some evidence first, see where it points to."

Rex straightened his posture. "Tonight?"

"No time like the present."

SEVEN

According to a tatty old telephone directory found in the desk drawer, John Laing lived in a small village west of Cloisterham called Buckchurch. His house sat off a village green next to a row of shops from the butchers to the post office. Since business hours were over, Rex and Eddie had the area to themselves. Eddie parked across from Laing's house, and they sat in the car.

"Do we knock?" Rex said.

"What would we do when he opened the door? Hello John, did you kill Derek?"

"How about, where were you on the night of October twenty-eighth?"

Eddie stared.

"Well, I'm open to suggestions."

"We need something solid that connects him to the murder."

"What's more solid than a confession?"

"We need to be more subtle. Softly, softly, catchee monkey, remember?"

Rex used binoculars his nan gave him to check out the

Laing residence, a large home with a long driveway. In the living room window, he saw Laing, tall with a grey beard, reading in a chair.

Rex folded his arms. "So now we just wait?"

"I thought you'd always wanted to do a stakeout."

"So did I, but this is rubbish. I'm hungry."

"I told you to bring snacks. Did you?"

"No. Did you?"

Eddie pulled his lunchbox closer. "For myself."

"I'm not sharing my cola then."

"I don't drink cola. It's dehydrating."

Rex scrunched up his face. "Don't get started with that again."

"It's true. It's science."

"It's science," Rex said in a caveman voice. "How can liquid dehydrate you? It's liquid."

Rex downed a two-litre bottle of cola in spite of Eddie. Since he couldn't believe someone didn't want to drink cola, this was the biggest revenge he could think of.

As he chugged away, Eddie clicked record on his voice-recorder. "Seven thirty-two p.m., subject is home."

Rex gasped with satisfaction and dropped the empty bottle. "What are you doing?"

"Documenting the evening."

"Why?"

"Because that's what detectives do."

"I don't know, I've watched plenty of movies and I've not seen that."

"Real life is more … methodical. It's dull, but it pays."

Rex crossed his arms even tighter.

"Seven thirty-three. Suspect moves to the kitchen, probably making dinner."

Eddie opened his lunchbox.

Rex pouted. "I'm so hungry."

"You should have thought about that before we left."

"What do you have?"

"I've got a tuna sandwich and a Scotch egg."

Rex bit his bottom lip. "Oh, I'd love a dirty Scotch egg right now."

"It's not dirty."

"It's a boiled egg, wrapped in sausage meat, covered in breadcrumbs. It's the dirtiest food ever."

"Eyes off my egg."

Rex grabbed the voice-recorder. "Seven thirty-three p.m. Eddie is being tight."

Eddie snatched it back. "Seven thirty-four p.m. Rex is ill-prepared and needs to take responsibility for himself."

Rex nabbed the recorder. "Seven thirty-five p.m. Eddie obviously isn't hungry, or he'd have finished eating by now. He's just being greedy."

Eddie and Rex wrestled the recorder as they shouted down the microphone.

"Seven thirty-five p.m. Rex needs to stop perving on my egg."

"Seven thirty-six p.m. I've never seen someone eat so slow."

"That's because Rex eats like a wolf."

"It's instinct. That's how people are meant to eat. I'll show you. Give me that sandwich."

"Get your own."

Rex dropped the recorder, and the pair tugged the sandwich to and fro. Eddie lost his grip. The extra force caused Rex to throw the sandwich over his shoulder. It hit the passenger window with a splat and slid down the glass. Rex scooped up the remains with his hands.

"I don't mind," Rex said. "This is how people are meant to eat. Clean plates are only a hundred years old."

"Oh really?"

Rex rebuilt the sandwich and picked off the carpet fuzz. "Before that you'd eat off more natural things like rocks, and leaves, and, uh—"

"Car doors?"

To spare another argument, and the car's upholstery, Eddie scoffed his Scotch egg.

Rex tapped his fingers on the empty bottle. "I need the toilet."

"Well, you shouldn't have downed that entire cola."

"Can you drive me to a petrol station?"

"No, one of us has to keep an eye on Laing. This is the countryside. Just go out and pee on a bush."

Rex surveyed the darkness. "I can't do it. I need a real toilet."

"It's how people are meant to pee," Eddie told him. "Toilets aren't even two hundred years old."

Rex looked out the window and back at Eddie with pursed lips. "I'll wait."

"This isn't very fruitful," Eddie said. "So far we've learnt John Laing likes a late dinner, doesn't brush his teeth for the full three minutes, and likes to read into the night. Let's take shifts until something interesting happens."

A coin toss gave Eddie the first nap. When Eddie awoke, he was overcome by his stiff neck.

"Rex, how long did I sleep?" No answer. "Rex?" He looked over to the passenger seat: Rex was gone. He wasn't in the backseat either. "Where the hell is he?"

Eddie called Rex's mobile phone and got the same answer message he'd had for twelve years. The recording was so old Rex's voice hadn't fully broken at the time he recorded it. It was an octave or two off, and well past its cultural relevance.

"Whassup! This is Rex Milton. Leave a message."

"It's Eddie. Where are you?" Eddie had to say his name because Rex had an old brick of a phone, too simple to connect the calling number to his contacts.

Eddie needed to think like a detective. *If I was Rex,* he thought. *Where would I be? He needed the bathroom; he won't go outside. He'd go to the nearest bathroom, which is … John Laing's house?* A burdening worry wrapped around Eddie's skull. *He couldn't.*

With the lights off in Laing's house, Eddie guessed he must be asleep. Rex would be either inside or trying to get in around the back.

Eddie ran, low and fast, to Laing's six-foot-high wooden fence. He jumped up and grabbed the top of the fence with his fingers. As he pulled himself up, he tore his trousers against a loose nail.

At the top of the fence, Eddie was overcome with dizziness and exhaustion. He promised to join a gym once they got the reward money. Since a membership felt too expensive, he haggled himself down to a new pair of trainers, but he persuaded himself to wait until the old ones wore out. At his current rate of exercise, that would be sometime next year. All this self-justification gave Eddie enough time to catch his breath.

The dizziness returned when Eddie realised the jump was six-foot, four-foot with his legs hanging. He'd never jumped from that height before and thought he had the right to be a little worried.

People break legs tripping at ground level, he thought.

A car driving down the street spooked Eddie, and he jumped. The landing was ninety percent successful. When he got up and walked, his ankle had a click. It didn't hurt, but the clicking was creepy. Eddie snuck around to the back in total darkness.

"Rex?" he shout-whispered. He heard steps on the pebbled path, then nothing. "Come on, stop messing about."

A black Staffordshire Bull Terrier stepped into the moonlight.

"Nice boy?"

The dog barked. Eddie ran back to the side and climbed the fence door. At the top, he leaned forward, and his weight pushed the unlocked door open. His head smacked into the brick wall.

Eddie hadn't thought to check the door; he'd assumed it was locked. He hated convenient moments in movies, especially when someone steals a car and finds the keys in the visor. As the door swung him head first into the brick wall, Eddie learnt he hated inconvenient moments more.

The dog stood outside between him and the car. It barked and scratched at the bottom of the fence door. Eddie took off a shoe and waved it at the dog. The hound's head bobbed with the movement. Eddie threw the shoe into the back garden.

"Fetch."

Eddie jumped as the dog chased after the shoe. He landed on the same dodgy ankle in a way that fixed the clicking.

Finally, something convenient, he thought.

The dog raced back with the shoe. Eddie slammed the door shut and took a deep breath. The whole fence pushed back as the dog jumped at the door. Eddie scurried back to the car, his shoeless foot hobbling along the pebbled driveway. Eddie approached the car, and his exposed foot splashed into a muddy puddle.

"Oh, come off it."

With the driver door open, Eddie shook his bare foot dry, or dryish, and twisted the brown water out of his sock. He slumped back into the driver's seat, and the rear-view mirror caught Eddie's eye. In the reflection, he saw a pub by the village square. That's where Rex would be.

EIGHT

Eddie entered the pub and searched for Rex. A low Tudor ceiling, black wooden beams, and mismatched furniture created a labyrinth lit by a warm fireplace. Grey-haired tubby men sat at separate tables enjoying a lone pint. From the bar, Eddie heard Rex's laughter, the only real sign of life. He marched towards the noise until he turned a corner and saw Rex drinking with their suspect, John Laing.

Eddie walked to the bar, ordered himself an orange juice, and waited. The clock above said it was ten forty-three p.m. Eddie had slept for over two hours.

God knows what damage Rex could have caused in that time, he thought.

Eddie nervously sipped his orange juice until Rex finished his drinks and approached the landlord.

"Same again, please."

Eddie shook his head. "What do you think you're playing at?"

Rex smiled. "And whatever my friend is having."

"Drinking with the suspect, you are unbelievable."

"Genius, right?"

"Are you mad? He's a potential killer, and you've revealed yourself."

"It's okay," Rex leaned in, "I'm undercover."

"Rex," Laing called out.

"With your own name?"

"Rex is a common name."

"Rex Milton, get over here," Laing shouted.

"I'm coming, mate."

"I can't believe you did this."

"It's one drink, plus I'm getting leads out of him."

"Like what?"

Rex wobbled forward. "Getting, not got. It's a process."

"You're drunk."

"It's all part of the process," Rex slurred.

"How's that?"

Rex pointed to Laing. "He's drunk too."

Eddie's eyes flashed. "Wait, this could work. He's at a disadvantage, he might let something slip."

After introductions, where Rex christened Eddie with the undercover name Eddie, the three drank and talked.

"So, Rex says you wrote for TV."

"He does. How does he know that?"

"Uh, you told me, a minute ago," Rex said.

"I did." Laing held the drink up to his face. "How much have I had to drink?" He shrugged and took another sip. Rex tipped Laing's glass higher to pour more down the man's throat.

Rex put on a fake grin. "You were talking about that Derek Lawrence man."

"Oh no, I am drunk. I don't like to talk about him. The whole thing left a nasty taste in my mouth."

Rex nodded. “Made you mad, did it? Vengeful perhaps?”

Eddie kicked Rex in the shin.

“What do you do now?” Eddie said.

“I own a software company. I just collect the cheques, but the company makes accounting software.”

“That reminds me, Eddie, we’re gonna need to talk expenses later.” Rex pointed at the many empty glasses on the table.

“What accounting software?”

“Oh, it’s too dull to talk about.”

“Dull, eh?” Rex said. “Where do you get your thrills from?”

Eddie kicked him again. “Sorry? He’s being weird. So, why’d you get out of TV?”

“Derek Lawrence,” Rex said. “Duh.”

“How’d you know that?” Laing said.

Eddie kicked a third time.

Laing grimaced. “Ouch.”

“Sorry.” Eddie tried again, this time he got Rex in the shin.

“Owww.”

Laing wagged a finger at Eddie. “What are you playing at?”

“Uh, I’ve got Tourette's of the foot. Every now and then my leg spasms out like that. I can’t control myself.”

Rex glanced under the table. “Is that how you lost a shoe?”

“I’ve never heard of it,” Laing said.

“Yes, well, that’s the way diseases are, aren’t they? You never really hear about one until a celebrity gets diagnosed.”

Rex nodded, satisfied with the answer. Laing raised an eyebrow with scepticism.

Eddie sipped his orange juice. "You were talking about Derek Lawrence."

"Was I? That piece of work. He drove my show into the ground."

"And that made you mad?" Eddie asked.

"Yeah, I care about original stories. He was a rip-off merchant."

"You were producing partners though?"

"I didn't tell you that."

Eddie clenched his neck muscles. "Uh, you mentioned it earlier."

"No, I didn't."

"He did, didn't he, Rex?"

Rex's eyes darted between Eddie and Laing. His conflict-induced fear-freezing kicked in once again.

"Rex?"

"This is between you guys."

"What is this?" Laing said.

"What's what?" Eddie asked.

"I see what's going on here."

"Uh, you do?"

"You're from that bloody message board, aren't you? As I told the last fan, I don't like to talk about Derek Lawrence. I've moved on. I don't care about the show. And I don't know what the characters would be up to today, but if you must know, half of them would probably be dead by now."

Eddie nudged Rex and smiled. "That's what I said."

Rex snapped out of his frozen state. "Now that Lawrence is dead, do you regret the way things turned out?"

"I only regret one thing, saying yes to working with the git. That man knew nothing about character. He was a journo who got lucky when the rights to his book were picked up. He wasn't a fiction writer. That's why he never worked again. Because he couldn't come up with an original story. He just read the newspaper and stole from it."

"You still seem pretty mad about it," Eddie said.

Laing curled his top lip. "What are you getting at?"

"Did you kill Derek Lawrence?" Rex said.

"Rex!"

"Where were you on the night of October twenty-eighth?"

"Stop talking, Rex," Eddie begged.

Laing stared at the pair. His face emotionless. He took a slow sip of his drink. He grinned and let out a chuckle. Rex chuckled with him. Laing's reaction turned into a belly laugh. Rex joined in. Their laughter escalated until they both cried. They laughed for so long, Eddie squirmed at the idea they were laughing at him.

Laing stood up. "You boys ask some weird questions. I'm gonna take a potty break." He wobbled to the men's room as his laugh calmed down.

Eddie leaned in. "What's funny?"

"I don't know," Rex said in a panic. "I was laughing because he was laughing."

"This is a dead end. Laing's got no motive for killing Lawrence. He's moved on. What a waste of time."

Rex finished his beer and let out a burp.

"And a waste of money," Eddie said.

The bar bell rang. "Time gentleman, please," called the landlord.

"You paid yet?"

"No, they said we could pay at the end. I love country folk."

"Let's go."

"Leave? But John—"

Eddie grabbed Rex's shoulder. "Can afford it."

As Laing left the men's room, he saw Rex and Eddie pass by.

"Leg it," Eddie shouted.

"Bye John," Rex said as Eddie pulled him through the door.

In the morning, Eddie picked up Rex, and they drove to the office.

"I've been thinking about what Laing said."

"Eddie, I really think the message board doesn't want to know about the characters being dead."

"Not that. He said Lawrence based his stories on what he read in the newspaper. If we get our hands on what he was writing when he died, we could find out what he was involved in, and possibly a motive."

"You think someone killed him for writing about them?"

"Maybe. The only problem is, I don't know how to get our hands on what he wrote."

Rex's eyes lit up. "The filing cabinet in our office."

"We had his writing, and you didn't say anything?"

"I said, what do you want me to do with all this paper, and you said chuck it."

Eddie tightened his grip on the steering wheel. "You threw it out?"

"No."

"Thank God."

"I got Harold the cleaner to do it."

Eddie put his foot down, which gave the car just

enough oomph to speed up a few extra miles per hour. They rushed into the office and pulled the filing cabinet's top drawer open. A lone pencil rolled to the front. All four drawers were empty.

Eddie stared at Rex. "Guess someone's gonna have to go through the wheelie bin."

The wheelie bin was full of used packages, papers, Styrofoam cups, and rotten food. Rex jumped right in without hesitation and searched for Lawrence's writings. Each time he swirled the contents around, he'd release new smells.

Eddie held out a black bin bag as Rex pulled stacks of papers from the mess and chucked them into the bag. Harold wandered out the office building and lit a cigarette. He noticed Eddie standing with the open bin bag.

"What the bleedin' hell are you doing?"

Eddie forced a smile. "Uh, nothing."

Rex popped out of the wheelie bin and dropped another load of papers. The weight of the documents blew the bag's smelly air into Eddie's face.

"That took me ages," Harold said.

"I'm sorry. We made a mistake," Eddie said.

"You're gonna get me in trouble climbing around in that wheelie bin."

"Again, I'm sorry. How'd you carry all the papers down?" Eddie said.

"I loaded up my wheelbarrow and rolled it down the stairs."

"I couldn't borrow your wheelbarrow could I?"

"Nope. I left it at home, but you can have me last bin liner."

"Uh, this is your last bin liner."

"Bleedin' cheek."

"Sorry."

After Rex filled the bag, Eddie carried it up to the office and poured the paper on the floor. Eddie dumped the third round of documents as the sound of a reversing lorry grew louder. Out the window, Eddie saw the bin men had come to empty the wheelie bin. As their lorry beeped towards the container, Eddie worried about Rex's habit of freezing in troublesome situations. In a panic, he pulled on the window to shout out, but it was still stuck. He raced down the stairs. As Eddie exited the back of the building, the lorry's hoist clung to the sides of the wheelie bin.

"Stop!"

They couldn't hear Eddie as the lorry rumbled and beeped. He ran to the nearest bin man, but the man didn't hear anything with his ear protectors on. Eddie jumped and waved. The bin man had seen his fair share of nutters and waddled away unfazed. Eddie grabbed the bin man's collar; at that point, Eddie realised just how tall the bin man was. He hadn't planned any further than grabbing the collar. Before Eddie came up with a decent idea, the bin man shoved him back. Eddie flew four-foot before he hit the concrete.

On his backside, Eddie screamed as the lorry's hoist lifted the wheelie bin. It rained bin bags, soiled cardboard and empty paper cups so fast he thought he saw Rex fall, but couldn't be sure.

Eddie jumped up, shoved past the bin man, and rushed to the compactor button. With a clank and thunk, the Lorry's compactor crushed down. He was too late. Eddie reached the end of the truck and watched in horror while the lorry squashed its insides.

"Eddie," a happy voice called out. "They let me push the button." Eddie turned his head and a delighted Rex waved from the compactor button. The rest of the papers were tucked under his arm.

Eddie turned red. "I'm gonna kill you, you stupid bastard." The bin men gathered around Rex with their arms folded like he was part of their posse. Eddie backed away with his arms in the air.

Rex smiled. "It's okay. We're best friends."

The bin men calmed down and shook Eddie's hand as a sign of peace. When Eddie got back in the office, he washed his hands three times before the smell disappeared, and twice more before he was satisfied.

"This is it," Rex said. "This is the story we've been looking for."

After shuffling papers all day, they'd only read a third of Derek Lawrence's stories. Eddie took the paper and scanned it.

"The young boy snatched the VHS tape and ran out the shop," Eddie read. "A shoplifter? Not quite murder level revenge. It's maybe enough to warrant a strongly worded letter."

"Fine." Rex chucked the story into what he'd dubbed, "The Nope Pile."

Eddie sprayed air freshener around the office. The papers had been in the wheelie bin long enough to stew in the juices and filth of everything else thrown in there. Unable to open the window, they took hourly breaks from the smell to spray half a bottle of Lavender Meadow.

Eddie picked up a scruff of a letter. It said: *Dear Derek*

Lawrence, thank you for your most recent writing submission, The Chukka Boot Killer. We would be interested in representing you and your novel.

"This is promising. Rex, search for anything with the words Chukka Boot Killer. The story got him an agent nine months ago. If he was close to publishing a real case, then that could have earned him an enemy."

Four more hours and a Chinese takeout later, the pair found pages to Lawrence's Chukka Boot Killer manuscript.

Eddie read an excerpt aloud, "The Chukka Boot Killer wrapped his leather glove around the brass door handle. After a slow twist, he shoved the door wide open. In a second, he fired his bullet, and the accountant died at his desk. Not a second to see his killer, not a moment for his life to flash by"

"What's a chukka boot?" Rex said. He typed it into the search engine and pressed enter. "The chukka boot is a desert boot usually made of suede."

Eddie stood over Rex's shoulder. "Search Chukka Boot Killer."

"It says here there is a gangster named Terry Palmer who made a name for himself in the late seventies. He was known for wearing his chukka boots."

"Did he ever visit Cloisterham?"

"He's from here." Rex read aloud, "He's a brutally violent man who hammers nails into his victims because bullets killed them too quickly. Ah crap. That's not how Derek Lawrence was killed."

"No, but if he wanted to get away with it, he'd kill in a different way."

"Oh yeah," Rex perked up, "this is excellent."

"I'll stick with crap," Eddie said. "This isn't someone we want to get on the wrong side of."

"Chill out, Eddie. This is the best news we've had all day."

Eddie took over the mouse and scrolled through the information. "He has an autobiography, but I doubt he wrote a confession in it."

The door knocked, putting Rex and Eddie on edge. Harold poked his head in.

"Come to empty your bins."

He surveyed the wet and stained papers covering the floor. The only spot free of soggy paper was the empty wastepaper basket.

Eddie lowered his head in shame. "We're good thanks." Harold flared his nostrils as he closed the door.

Rex hurried to the doorway. "Harold? Do you know anything about Terry Palmer?"

Harold leaned back in the office chair. Rex and Eddie sat on the floor with their legs crossed.

"Bootsy, they call him. He's a horrible bastard. You'll never see him without those boots. I was told he even wore them at his wedding. Top hat, coattails and chukka boots. The only time Palmer was caught without them was when he was caught with not much else."

Rex's eyebrows lifted. "He was naked?"

"The police found him walking down East Cloisterham High Street in nothing but his boxer briefs. They wanted a word with him because his brother Danny was murdered that night. Shot in the back of the head while working on his accounts."

"He was his accountant?" Rex asked.

"Business partner. Terry did the crimes, and Danny

funnelled the dirty money into legitimate businesses. So the rumours go."

"Sorry," Eddie said. "Why was he in just his underwear?"

"It was such a mess the killer would have been covered in Danny Palmer's blood. They had footprints in the blood too. Just needed to find the boots."

"Like Cinderella?" Rex said.

"Bootsy walked away from it all. Since they found him without clothes or boots, they had nothing on him."

Rex nudged Eddie. "Literally."

"Why would he kill his brother? He'd lose his ability to move his money?"

"They went legit. Danny invested in an African diamond mine for them, and they were set. With Danny gone, Terry became the sole owner."

"What a bastard," Rex said.

Harold nodded. "I told you, didn't I?"

"Not one witness saw Palmer covered in blood?" Eddie said.

"His wife was his alibi. Said they'd got in an argument in bed, and he was kicked out before he could put his trousers on. Police asked him where he was going, and he told them he was off to the pub."

"What did you know about Derek Lawrence?"

"Quiet man. He was divorced, I think. He was here every day seven a.m. to seven p.m. Twenty years."

"Every day?" Eddie said.

"Every day."

"Even Christmas?" Rex said.

"Every bleedin' day. I'd empty his bin on Christmas Eve, and it would be full of paper Boxing Day morning."

"Did his daughter ever come by?"

"I never met her. This was his Shangri-La."

Eddie gave the damp-stained walls a once-over. "Some Shangri-La."

"You boys detectives then?"

Eddie shrugged. "Kind of."

"Yes," Rex said with a firm nod. "We are."

"You're not police though?"

Rex grinned. "We're private detectives."

"You going to solve the Danny Palmer murder are you?"

"I guess so," Rex said.

"No, we're just collecting some information on Derek Lawrence's death."

"Come on, Eddie. It'll be good for business. Two murders are better than one."

"You reckon Terry Palmer offed Lawrence, do yah?" Harold let out a raspy laugh. "They didn't exactly hang out in the same circles."

"Lawrence must have had something on him. We found one page of a manuscript about a killer with boots."

"You boys'd be better off dumping these papers and getting another case. A lost bicycle, something like that seems more like your cup of tea."

"We've got one more question," Rex said.

Eddie knew Rex's question and shook his head. "No, we don't."

"Where were you on the night of October twenty-eighth?"

Harold shook his head and walked himself out. "What a bleedin' sorry pair you are."

Eddie stood up. "We need to gather every page on Palmer. Lawrence knew something that spooked him. We just need to find it. You start going through the papers for anything supporting our theory. I'll order a pizza."

"Pizza and Chinese food? On the same day?" Rex smiled wide enough to flash his teeth.

"Yeah, let's treat ourselves. At this rate, we'll have our five grand tomorrow."

Eddie awoke rejuvenated. He gave the Morris Minor a full tank of petrol and headed to The Octagon's shoe shop. He peered through the shop glass to check Melinda was there and strutted inside.

Melinda gave a forced smile. "Eddie. How are you?"

"I'm looking for new shoes."

"Please, you can't check up on me like this."

"I don't know what you're talking about. I'm here for shoes."

"It's just, I heard you got fired and, I don't want you to blow your money on buying shoes to see me."

"This is strictly professional, Melinda. If you can't keep your feelings for me separate, I guess I'll get my footwear from somewhere else."

Eddie turned to the door.

"Fine, what kind of shoes are you looking for?"

He turned back with a grin. "Well, I'm a successful business owner now. I need shoes that say I've made something of myself, that I'm going places. Do you sell those kinds of shoes?"

Melinda looked Eddie up and down. He looked pretty slick in his suit, but the socks and sandals combination let him down.

"What happened to your other shoes?"

Eddie lowered his voice to a mumble. "I lost one of them."

"Pardon?"

Eddie pointed at a pair on display. "Those shoes are sharp. Is that three hundred each?"

"For the pair."

"Oh, what a… bargain."

Melinda smiled. "What's got into you?"

"Nothing much, just solved a case that's all."

"Like a detective?"

"Oh, I didn't tell you? Me and Rex have a detective agency. We solved a big case, and today we pick up five thousand pounds."

"Wow. That's exciting."

"Not bad for a couple of days work."

"That's a lot of money."

"Is it?" Eddie smiled.

Melinda stepped closer and her voice softened. "You seem different, Eddie."

"Just going out there, taking risks, and, uh, getting. Like a go-getter."

She grinned. "It's good on you."

"I want those shoes, the three hundred pound ones. Those are the shoes a man should pick up five grand in."

"You know what you want. I like it."

"I was wondering, Melinda, if you'd like to go get dinner, maybe this evening?"

"Where?"

Eddie smiled. "It's a surprise."

"Exciting. Yeah, okay."

Eddie picked up Rex, and they drove to Snodling to visit Stacey Lawrence. They had left her a message early in the morning to say they had the evidence. She called back and arranged for them to come over right away.

"Come in," Stacey said, wide-eyed and a little nervous. Rex and Eddie shuffled in ready to share their wisdom. They followed her down the corridor to the living room. The pair's cocksure strut was disrupted when Rex tripped on an unzipped backpack, spilling a pair of ballet shoes. He tiptoed so as not to tread on the slippers, but bumped into a framed painting instead.

"Sorry."

Eddie shook his head and followed Stacey into the living room. Rex and Eddie took a seat opposite Stacey.

"Your father was murdered," Eddie said.

"Yes, I know that."

"We learnt he wrote a novel about a gangster who killed an accountant. The gangster is a thinly disguised version of Terry Palmer, have you heard of him?"

"The boots guy, right?"

"Bootsy," Rex said.

Eddie leaned forward. "He was a suspect in the murder of his brother in nineteen-seventy-nine. He wasn't charged as the police had no evidence. On the night of the murder, Bootsy was found without his clothes."

"What's this got to do with Dad?"

Rex handed her the collected pages of Lawrence's writing.

"Your father's novel was about a journalist who witnesses a killer dump his blood-soaked clothes into the river. We believe your father wrote about his real-life experiences. He witnessed Palmer hide the evidence that could have put him away for life."

"So how'd this man find out about the book? Dad never published anything."

"No, but he sent out the manuscript to many publishers. It seems he targeted anyone that had previously published a crime book."

Rex handed over the acceptance letter they found.

"This letter shows he sent it to P&P Publishing, which stands for Palmer & Palmer. Terry Palmer set up his own publishing company with his then-wife in nineteen-ninety-eight to release his vanity project, an autobiography."

"That was a mistake," Rex said.

"We believe Palmer heard about the query letter, recognised the plot, and asked for the manuscript. He read it and had your father killed."

Stacey reviewed the papers, one by one, with her hand over her mouth.

Rex cleared his throat. "Did we do good?"

"Give her a minute."

She paled. "Did you go to the police?"

Rex shook his head. "No, we came straight here."

"Do we go to the police?" Eddie asked.

Stacey straightened the papers. "I'll take care of it."

"In that case, you can check over the evidence. All we need is the reward money."

"Of course, I can have it for you tomorrow morning."

"Not now?"

"I need some time, you only called an hour ago. Come back tomorrow morning. It's not like you don't know where I live."

The pair got into the Morris Minor. As Eddie drove along the country road, he noticed Rex stare out the window.

"Well done, Rex. We solved the case."

Rex struggled to find the words as he put on his seat-belt. "It's just, it's not what I expected. I wanted a femme fatale, a couple of double crossings, a big reveal, you know, a car chase."

"Sorry Rex, but real detective work is time-consuming and monotonous." He started the car and drove down the country lane. “In real life, it’s hard work and due diligence that pays off. Now let’s get a beer.”

Rex perked up. “Uh, Eddie.”

“It’s okay. There's no need to thank me.”

“No, it’s just, well, a black SUV is following us.” Rex pointed at the rear-view mirror. Eddie saw the black SUV catch up to them. He didn’t know what was worse: the thought of being followed, or that Rex was excited about it.

NINE

As Eddie drove down the lane, his focus darted between the road ahead, and the black SUV in the rear-view mirror.

"It's following us," Rex said. "Five minutes and he's still behind us. That's following."

"I'm sure we're just sharing the only road back into town."

Rex patted the dashboard. "Speed up."

"We are not having a car chase. Get over it."

"Do some weird turns, and see if you lose him?"

"There aren't any turnings," Eddie snapped. "It's a country lane." His agitation increased as his breathing became shallow.

"There, turn into those houses."

"Fine. But only to prove to you that he's just another driver headed to Cloisterham."

Eddie turned left. Both of them watched the rear-view mirror. The black SUV turned after them.

"Ah ha!" Rex said.

"Doesn't prove anything." Eddie turned right and left

again. He then pulled into to an empty parking space and waited. No SUV.

Eddie sighed relief. "See?"

"Damn, he's good."

"Give it a rest."

Eddie pulled the car out and joined the main road. Within a minute they were back in town with steady traffic. The black SUV appeared behind them, a little further back this time.

"He's behind us again."

"What?" Eddie checked his rear window. There it was.

"Told you he was good."

"It's a coincidence."

"We stopped for a full minute, and he still managed to be behind us."

"Maybe he stopped for petrol or something." Eddie put his foot down, and the Morris Minor crept towards 43 mph.

"Speed up."

"This is sped up for uphill."

"Uphill? This is a slope."

Eddie thumped his foot down. The car spluttered up to 50 mph.

Rex adjusted his glasses and checked the speedometer. "Is this thing even in the right gear?"

"Yes, thank you."

As the road evened out, the car reached 55 mph.

"School crossing," Rex called out.

A lollipop lady stepped out into the road holding a stop sign. Eddie put his foot on the brake, and a clank sound rang from beneath them.

Eddie's eyes widened. "That doesn't sound healthy."

They were headed downhill towards the zebra crossing. The Morris Minor increased speed going 56, 57, 58 mph.

Eddie honked the horn, but the stubborn lollipop lady wouldn't budge. He held his foot down on the brake so hard his ankle spasmed. Eddie thumped the car horn, which squeaked and squealed at a higher pitch with each hit. As they headed for the crossing, he swerved into the other lane and passed the lollipop lady.

"That was brilliant." Rex pumped his fist in the air.

They both looked back to see the lollipop lady give them the finger, as the black SUV hurried past her and accelerated towards the Morris Minor.

Honk! Honk!

Eddie swung his head forward. They headed towards a collision with an oncoming lorry. He pulled back into the right lane as the lorry brushed past. Its roaring engine blew hot air into Eddie's face.

"That was not brilliant," Eddie said.

Rex looked back. "SUV's still following us."

"I see that." He shifted from third to fifth gear. The car made a noise like it cleared its throat and coasted along the street. "Uh, I think the clutch is gone." The car came to a slow crawl as the slope flattened out. Eddie used the last of their momentum to pull the car to the curb.

"What are you doing?" Rex said. "He's gonna catch us now."

The black SUV raced past them.

Eddie shrugged. "I guess he was just in a hurry too."

"Yeah, right. That's what he wants us to think."

"Let's calm down."

Rex raised his palms. "You're right. We need to take a moment to process our first car chase."

"I don't think that counts as a car chase. It was more like, tandem speeding."

Eddie sat in the tow truck with his arms folded tight. He stared forward, perched between the driver and Rex.

The stupid Morris Minor, Eddie thought, *with its dodgy brakes, broken clutch, and pathetic wooden structure.*

"Left at the next light," he said, only talking to bark directions.

Rex winced. "Eddie, are you sure this is a good idea?"

"Left."

"Eddie?"

They pulled up outside Tim's house. Eddie paid the driver as he lowered the Morris Minor into the road.

"Between the blown out tyre and now the clutch, we've spent a quarter more than the sales price on this stupid lump of metal. We've only got four-hundred and thirty-five pounds left."

Rex put on a friendly smile. "Are you okay?"

"I will be when we've got our money from Tim. Getting three-quarters of our money back is better than keeping that junk."

"You want to sell back the car?"

"I want justice."

Eddie marched to Tim's door, and Rex bounded along to keep up.

The red BMW was gone. Instead, a black 2007 Mercedes Benz C-Class was on the driveway.

Rex gazed at the car. "Now that's a sweet ride."

Eddie knocked. The door opened and a middle-aged woman, with mousy-blonde hair collected in a scrunchy, took a drag of her cigarette and blew in their direction.

She drew her top lip back in a snarl. "What?"

Eddie gave a polite smile. "Hello. Is Tim in?"

"Who's asking?"

Rex waved. "Rex and Eddie. Hello."

"Whatcha want?"

"I need to speak to him about the car we bought," Eddie said.

"I ain't got nothing to do with that."

"I know, that's why I want to talk to Tim."

"What about the car?" she said.

"It's broken," Eddie said.

"You want him to fix your motor?"

"I'd rather just have my money back."

"You'll have to talk to him about that."

"Yes, that's what I've been trying to tell you."

She blew smoke at the pair. Rex smiled to break the tension.

"He ain't here."

"Where is he?"

"Out."

"Does he own the Benz?" Rex said.

"Yeah."

"What happened to the BMW?"

"He totalled it, didn't he? He crashed it, and the insurance gave him ten grand for it. He only got it for five, but it was undervalued, see. So now he's got this."

"Nice."

"His dad ain't happy." She took another puff. "It's better than his motor."

"Where is Tim?" Eddie said.

"At work with his uncle. Regal Repairs, the mechanics."

Eddie remembered that name. He stomped to the car and pulled the MOT certificate from the glove compartment.

"Damn it."

"What's up, Eddie?"

"Regal Repairs did the MOT. Tim got his uncle to declare it roadworthy. The cheeky git fudged it."

"I'm sure this is all some misunderstanding," Rex called across the driveway. "Right, Mrs Tim's mum?"

"You'll have to talk to him about it."

She closed the door.

"Come on, Rex. We're going to the mechanics."

"Don't we need to wait for the tow truck?"

"I'm not spending another penny on that firewood on wheels. We'll push it."

Eddie unwound the driver window to control the steering as he pushed the car. Rex pushed from the back. Within a quarter of a mile the novelty wore off.

"Eddie, this isn't fun anymore."

"It's not meant to be fun. Now, push. We'll reach a roundabout in a minute and we need a running start if we're gonna make it."

Rex found the journey across the roundabout a bit hairy at times. Ever the optimist, he focused on how Eddie's anger managed to wipe away any trace of anxiety. He liked Eddie taking charge, even though he'd turned an unhealthy shade of red in the process.

They pulled the car into the Regal Repairs garage, which was more of a tin shed. A bald man with a grey beard lay under a bonnet and tugged wires out of its engine.

Eddie cleared his throat.

The bald man sat up. "What?"

"Is Tim here?"

Tim glided out from under the car holding an engine part. He looked it over and dumped it on the floor. When he saw Rex and Eddie, he smiled.

"How you boys doing?"

"Fine," Rex said.

"Not fine," Eddie said.

"Having a tiff, are we? Don't worry fellas. Love conquers all."

"The Morris Minor, it's falling apart."

"What you done to it?"

The bald man, Tim's uncle, positioned himself behind his nephew as he wiped his oily hands on his blue overalls.

"I haven't done anything. You sold me a shoddy vehicle." Eddie pointed at Tim's uncle. "And you wrote a bogus MOT."

The uncle puffed his chest out. "Is that right?"

"Yes." Eddie's voice rose an octave or two. He cleared his throat. "The clutch is gone, and the brakes aren't working."

"Wasn't like that when I sold it to you."

"It was fine when I did the MOT," the uncle said.

"Look, I don't want trouble. I just want my eight hundred back."

Tim sniggered. "Sorry mate, I ain't in the market."

"I'm not selling. I want a refund. Or I'll report this place."

Tim crossed his arms. "Clutch is wear and tear."

"I've not even done a hundred miles in it."

"Don't matter if it's ten or a hundred thousand," the uncle said. "It's the last mile that broke it. And I weren't at the wheel. Was you at the wheel Tim?"

"No, uncle," Tim said, glaring at Rex and Eddie.

"We can fix it up for you. For a discount."

Eddie grimaced. "How much of a discount?"

"Fifty percent."

The uncle replaced the clutch and brakes and brought up the total on the register.

"We spotted a few other things. All in all, it cost four-hundred-and-twenty-eight pounds."

"What about the discount? You said fifty percent."

"On labour. Can't give you a discount on parts. They ain't ours. I'd be working at a loss. Now, that ain't reasonable."

"So it's only reasonable if I'm the one losing is it?"

The uncle pounded his wrench into his palm. "You disrespecting me and my nephew?"

"Disrespect? No."

"'Cause it looks that way."

"I'm not."

"You're paying then?" the uncle asked.

Eddie sighed. "Yes, I'm paying."

He handed over the cash and marched to the Morris Minor. Eddie stepped in and slammed the door so hard the wing mirror dropped an inch. Rex silently slid into his seat. The engine started and they drove away from the sunset.

"I can't let them get away with that, Rex."

"You get your five grand tomorrow. You'll come out on top at the end of this adventure."

Eddie snarled. "I know a way to come out on top."

"Let's go have a drink and celebrate the end of the case."

"I've just got one thing to do."

They drove to the corner of Tim's street, where Eddie parked and opened the car's boot.

"Eddie, what are you doing?"

"Justice." Eddie lifted a leftover can of the office paint and stormed towards Tim's Mercedes-Benz.

Rex settled in his seat. "I think I'll wait in the car."

Eddie grabbed the lid of the paint, but he couldn't

open it. The dried paint had glued it shut. He pulled his keys from his pocket and wedged open the can. When he yanked the lid off drops of paint flew across the driveway and onto Eddie's new shoes.

"Ahhhh," Eddie groaned. He picked up the can and poured the paint all over the car's roof. The thick primer enveloped around the car and down the windows.

Eddie watched with glee. "No one messes with Eddie Miles," he muttered. "No one."

Tim's mother opened the door. "Are you mental?" she shouted. Eddie backed away into the darkness as she viewed the car. "What the hell?"

"Uh, excuse me." Eddie sprinted down the street to the Morris Minor, jumped in the car, and started the engine.

"What are you doing?" Rex said.

"Taking us to the pub." Eddie buckled his seatbelt. "We're celebrating."

With the car dropped off at the office, Rex and Eddie were free to get a celebratory beer in town.

Eddie raised his pint for a toast. "Despite Regal Repairs, it's been a great day. I'm ecstatic to say we solved a case."

"Indeed, chin chin."

The pair clicked their pint glasses together and downed a splash of booze.

"Seriously, Rex. I'm proud. We managed to catch a murderer. And we didn't have to go near him. We just used our brains and systematic processing of evidence. We didn't even get our hands dirty."

"What about when I was in the wheelie bin?"

"Yes, well then. But I mean in a figure of speech way, we didn't have to deal with Terry Palmer."

After a couple of beers, they left the pub and realised the sun had gone down. Both were in a state between being drunk enough not to need a coat while out in the cold, but not drunk enough that a reasonable person would take a taxi home.

"All right mate," said a voice in the darkness. It was Billy the Quid, the harmless beggar. He was tall, scraggly, and middle-aged, at least that was Eddie's estimate; homelessness ages people.

"Hello, Billy the Quid," Rex said. He never understood that wasn't Billy's real name, but what he was called behind his back.

"Can I borrow a pound?" Billy asked.

"Sorry, we're all out," Eddie said.

"Just one quid. I'll give it back."

"We got leftover pizza at the office," Rex offered. Billy frowned, thinking over their offer. This offended Eddie until he reminded himself the man's brain was fried, possibly from drugs; although, it may have been a stroke. Eddie didn't like to judge, but since he did, he assumed drugs.

Billy nodded. "Yeah, okay."

Eddie admired Rex's generosity; however, he was now stuck walking half a mile to the office with a homeless man. Rex could comfortably walk in silence, but Eddie always had to have small talk. Now he was stuck trying to work out what to talk to a homeless man about.

"Did you have a good day?" Eddie asked.

Billy shrugged. "It was okay. You?"

"I guess I did. We solved a crime today."

"Cool."

The silence returned, which killed Eddie.

Eddie sighed. "So, what do you do when you're not, uh, begging?"

"I'm not a beggar. I borrow money."

"Oh right, sorry. I guess it's like those microloans, huh? Micro-micro loans?" Billy didn't get the joke. Eddie couldn't find the right social context. "What do you do when you're not borrowing?"

"It's a full-time job. Doesn't leave much time for anything else. I do like politics though."

"Really? How'd you keep up to date with that?"

"The library. They got free books, free newspapers, free chairs, free toilets; you can even use the Internet for free. You follow politics."

"No," Eddie said with some embarrassment.

Everything was a conversational dead end. Billy occasionally broke silence to ask passing pedestrians for a pound. Eddie felt guilty that he and Rex ruined Billy's game a bit. The three of them made it more intimidating. One lady opened her purse to give Billy, Rex, and Eddie a pound each. They both gave theirs to Billy.

They arrived outside the office building, and Rex went in to grab the pizza. Niceties inclined Eddie to talk to Billy.

"You watch any sport?" Eddie asked.

"No."

"Yeah, me neither."

The silence continued. The street was quiet at this time of night. Eddie checked his phone. With no messages, emails or updates, he pretended to read to seem busy in front of Billy. As he fake typed, he was distracted by a noise, a whoosh, as if the wind shushed them.

"Did you hear that?" Eddie said. Billy looked confused, and a bit peeved. Red ran down his chest. "Billy?"

Billy fell to the ground, and Eddie crouched to try to catch him. A second whoosh, this time above Eddie's head, was followed by a chink sound. Behind him, the door's windowpane had spidered. The cracks in the glass led to a central bullet hole. Someone had shot at them. Eddie unlocked the door and barrelled into the office hallway as another bullet took out the intercom.

Rex ran down the stairs with the pizza box. He stopped when he saw Eddie crawl on the floor and bullets shattered the other window panels. Rex held the pizza box like a shield. Shots fired through the cardboard box and into the stairwell. He chucked the box and jumped over the railing towards Eddie. The pair shuffled on all fours to the back exit.

TEN

Rex and Eddie ran across the dark car park and jumped into the Morris Minor. Eddie started the engine and turned to Rex.

"Seat belt?" Eddie said.

"Are you serious?"

The metal clang of a bullet hitting the nearby lamp post rang across the car park.

"Safety first."

After Rex snapped in his seat belt, Eddie slammed his foot on the pedal. They didn't slow down until the office was a tiny dot in the rear-view mirror.

"Not bad for a car with a top speed of sixty-four miles-per-hour," Eddie said.

"Guess Tim's uncle really did fix us up proper," Rex said.

Eddie hung his head. "Well, yeah, I guess."

As Eddie drove, Rex called an ambulance for Billy. In the rear-view mirror reflection, Eddie saw the black SUV behind them.

"We're being followed."

Rex hung up the phone. "I know, but what do a bunch of mopeds want with us?"

Eddie checked his side mirror and found two mopeds in pursuit. In the passenger side mirror, another pair of scooters drew closer.

"Why're they following us," Eddie asked.

A green moped caught up to Eddie's window. In the driver's visor, a pair of narrowed eyes stared at Eddie.

"What's his problem?"

The moped came closer so the passenger was face-to-face with Eddie. The passenger lifted his visor. It was Tim. He gave Eddie the finger.

Rex waved. "Hi, Tim."

Tim's gang of scooters surrounded the Morris Minor, two on each side. They all kicked the car while driving.

"Hey," Eddie shouted. "This is dangerous."

Tim bashed Eddie's side mirror with his foot until the mirror snapped off. On Rex's side, the riders sprayed the car windows with spray paint. Rex stiffened.

"Rex, are you there?"

"Yes," he said through gritted teeth.

"Don't freeze up on me. I need you not to freeze up. In a second, I'm gonna tell you to run. You get out and follow me. Understood?"

Rex gulped. "Yes."

Eddie braked to a halt and the mopeds sped off. The riders' heads snapped back as they realised they'd lost the upper hand. One moped tried to hard break but skidded until it spun out on the ground. Eddie turned the car with a screech into a waiting zone parking spot outside Cloisterham Police Station.

"Run!"

They jumped out of the car and raced towards the police station entrance. Eddie's new shoes rubbed against the back of his heel as they ran. The mopeds turned around and roared back towards the station. Down the other end of the street, the black SUV skulked closer.

Rex and Eddie reached the automatic doors. They wouldn't open. Eddie waved at the sensor above the door. Rex jumped up and down on the mat.

"What are you doing?"

"I'm jumping so it will sense our weight."

"It's not automated by a scale, you idiot."

"Fine, we'll rely on your Jedi waves."

"I'm not being a Jedi. Just, look, look up there. That's a movement sensor."

Rex continued to jump as Eddie searched for a way inside. He spotted the open hours sign. It was just after nine o'clock and the station had closed.

"Just bloody perfect." Eddie threw his hands up in the air. "Due to cutbacks, this station will be open from nine a.m. to twelve p.m. and two p.m. to six p.m."

Rex stopped jumping. Through the glass door, Eddie saw a policeman exit the toilet and head down a corridor.

"They're in there." Eddie banged on the door. "They're inside."

Tim and his gang parked next to the Morris Minor. They used tools to smash up the car's lights and spray-painted graffiti on the side.

"We're on camera," Rex said. He jumped and waved at the security camera. Eddie watched the black SUV crawl up the street as the four teens peed on the Morris Minor in unison.

"The police aren't coming, Rex."

Tim and his gang sauntered towards them as Tim took off his helmet.

Eddie pantomimed a hint of recognition. "Tim, is that you?"

"You didn't know?" Rex said.

Eddie elbowed him to shut up.

Tim rolled back his shoulders. "Yeah, it's me."

"Thank goodness." Eddie placed his hand on his chest, pretending to be relieved. "I thought you were some random thugs. I see now it was all a misunderstanding. How are you doing?"

"You messed up my ride."

"I don't know what you're talking about."

"You poured paint on my Benz."

"Why would I do something like that?"

"I dunno." Tim cocked his head left and right, cracking his neck each time. "Deathwish?"

"Ha, ha. Good one. No seriously. Someone painted your car?"

"Not someone. You. I saw the paint can in your boot when I fixed your motor."

"Uh yes." Eddie bit his bottom lip. "And that paint was stolen, that's why we're here at the police station."

Rex winked at Eddie. "Yeah, stolen."

Tim pointed at Eddie's feet. "You got the same paint on your shoes."

Eddie glanced at the paint on his new shoes. "Oh that, yes well—" He ran to the station's glass door and bashed at it. "Help!"

Tim and his gang stepped forward.

Eddie swallowed. "They're just gonna let us die out here?"

"We just have to get their attention," Rex said.

"How?"

Rex's eyes widened. "Commit a crime?"

"We've got about ten seconds to get arrested before we're either beaten or shot, or both."

Rex let out a long, loud scream like a human horn.

Eddie covered his ears, shocked by Rex's unlimited source of air. Tim and the gang backed up, reading each other's faces. Rex waved his hands in a circle motion, egging on Eddie to join in. Eddie took a deep breath and gave it a go, but it turned into a high-pitch squeal, and he gave up.

The black SUV edged closer.

Rex took off his blazer and threw it on the floor. He undid his shirt and tossed it on the ground. The teens backed away.

"What are you doing?" Tim said.

Rex waved his arms and nodded at Eddie, encouraging him to follow suit. Eddie backed away as Rex threw his trainers at the security camera and unbuttoned his jeans.

"Sod this." Tim and his friends jumped on their mopeds and drove off. "You're freaks."

Tim's driver started the moped. As they drove past, Tim shouted, "I don't mean that in a gay way."

Their bikes hummed off past the approaching black SUV.

Rex jumped faster and shouted louder as he pulled his jeans down. The automatic door slid open and a police officer, tall and surly with a pencil moustache, stood on the other side. "What the hell do you think you're playing at?"

Rex stuck his arms out ready for the handcuffs. "Arrest us."

The officer flared his nostrils. "You want me to arrest you?"

"Yes, please."

Eddie nodded in agreement "A man is trying to kill us."

"I'll kill the pair of you, you carry on like this."

Rex buttoned his jeans back up and picked up his other items.

Eddie held his hands together like he was praying. "Please Officer, he shot at us, and he's following us." The black SUV drove by. "That's him in that car." The SUV carried on down the street.

The officer viewed over their heads. "Doesn't look like he's following you to me."

"Because we came here."

"What for?"

Eddie's jaw dropped. "Uh, Protection."

"You rang nine nine nine?"

"No."

"There is a standard procedure. You have to respect the procedure otherwise society would be madness."

"Please," Eddie begged, "can we come in."

"I don't think so, boys. You best be on your way."

Rex raised his hand. "They shot Billy the Quid."

The officer dismissed them with a shake of his head. "Of course they did."

"They did. We drove right here."

"That your parking is it?"

Eddie turned to the Morris Minor, wedged in the loading zone with its back end still in the street.

"Uh, no we came in a different car."

"What are you talking about, Eddie?"

"Now, you fellas be straight with me. You been drinking?"

"No," Eddie said.

Rex nodded. "Yes."

Eddie turned to Rex with clenched teeth. "No. We haven't."

Rex cocked his head in confusion. The officer watched them for a few seconds.

Eddie waved his hands in defeat. "He's been drinking. But I drove." The officer leaned in and smelt Eddie's breath. "Okay, it was two drinks, but I was under the limit, and I'm pretty sure the adrenaline from being shot at means I could drink an entire bottle of vodka, and still have my wits about me."

The officer stepped back into the station. "Clear off, the pair of you."

"Terry Palmer is trying to kill us," Eddie said. "You're not going to take that seriously?"

The officer leaned towards the pair. "Terry Palmer?"

"Yes."

"That's a serious accusation. You better come in."

Rex and Eddie stepped forward.

The officer raised his hand. "But not until he is fully dressed."

"So let me get this straight," the Detective Inspector said, "you're private detectives?"

"Yes." Rex nodded rapidly.

"Kind of," Eddie said. "Isn't this room for interviewing arrested people?"

"It's for recording purposes."

The Detective Inspector's name was Brown. He wore plain clothes, a suit with a dark blue raincoat. Brown had a youthful face, but the grey speckles of hair and yellowed eyes meant he was either a stressed young man, or an older man who moisturised. Eddie didn't think it was polite to ask.

Rex poked the audio recording machinery with curiosity. "This is cool."

Brown slapped Rex's hand away. "Don't touch. Can I see your P.I. Licence?"

Eddie gawked. "Pardon?"

"Your private detective licence."

"Pfft, we don't have one of those," Rex said.

Brown sighed, turned to the officer and grimaced. The officer shrugged his shoulders.

Rex thumped his fist on the table. "I demand to speak to the chief of police."

Brown focused on Eddie. "No licence?"

"On us," Eddie said. "We have one, of course. Are we, uh, meant to carry it on us?"

Rex could sense they were in trouble, but not what for. Feeling trapped in the room he neurotically scratched himself.

"What's wrong with him?" Brown asked as Rex furiously scratched his neck.

"He's fine. He's just nervous. So about us getting shot at—"

"I'm itchy."

Brown leaned back. "Should we be worried?"

"I should think so," Eddie said. "There's a murderer out there."

"I mean is the itching, contagious?"

Eddie shook his head. "No."

The officer crinkled his face in disgust. "Do we need to disinfect the interview room?"

"Can we please stick to the reason we are here?" Eddie asked.

"Indecent exposure," the officer said.

"No, Terry Palmer. Trying to kill us."

"Ah yes." Brown nodded. "Wasting police time."

"What? No, we were shot at." Eddie huffed. "Call the hospital. Check on Billy the Quid."

Brown turned to the officer.

"Billy the Quid is in the hospital with a bullet wound," the officer said.

"He'll corroborate our story."

Brown rested his hands on the table. "You want us to

treat a homeless man, who'll do anything for a pound, as a reliable witness?"

Rex furiously scratched his lower shoulder blade.

Eddie winced. "Yes, please?"

The officer sighed. "Billy is unconscious, and in a critical condition. We won't hear from him at all for the next few days."

"We could be killed by then," Eddie said.

Brown placed his elbows on the table. "You say Stacey Lawrence has all your evidence. You didn't back it up?"

"No. In hindsight, that would've been a good idea." Eddie turned to Rex and shook his head.

Rex raised his eyebrows. "What you looking at me like that for?"

"We tried contacting Miss Lawrence," Brown said. "She isn't at the address you gave, nor did she answer her phone."

"I bet she ran away as soon as she realised who murdered her father," Eddie said. "Are you still investigating that?"

"It was suicide," the officer said.

Eddie's mouth fell open. "He was shot in the back of the head. How is that suicide?"

"Do you know the percentage of deaths we've seen where it turns out the writer just killed themselves?" the officer said.

Eddie sneered. "No."

"Well, neither do we. But it's a lot. As in, a lot of writer deaths are suicide. In terms of Cloisterham's total deaths, there are very few writers committing suicide."

"I thought that was implied," Brown said.

"I didn't want them to think most deaths were writers."

Brown groaned. "Did you think that?"

Eddie lowered his voice to a mutter, "I don't think I should share what I'm thinking right now."

"Just so it is clear," the officer said. "Do you understand that although the percentage of writer deaths is low in the grand scale of deaths in Cloisterham, the number of writer deaths that turn out to be suicide is considered high."

"Are you finished?" Brown said.

"And those aren't exact numbers," the officer added.

Eddie's eyebrows lowered. "Those weren't numbers at all."

Brown stared at the officer. "Finished?"

"I just wanted to make sure I was understood?"

"Yes. I understand," Eddie said, exasperated.

Rex tilted his head. "I don't understand."

Eddie pointed at Rex while eyeballing Brown. "My advice is to let that slide."

The officer took a deep breath. "So, the deaths in Cloisterham are mostly made up of murders, manslaughters, accidents—"

"Please," Eddie said. "If you are going to insist on doing this, may I go to the toilet?"

Brown marched Eddie to the men's room. Once inside, Eddie thought something wasn't right. Maybe it was needing a potty break when his life was in danger. He thought adrenaline and testosterone were meant to take over, but here he was at the urinal.

When does Jack Bauer find time to use the bathroom? he wondered. *During the ad breaks?*

With his hands thoroughly washed, Eddie opened the door with a paper towel. In the hallway, Brown listened on his mobile phone. He raised his finger to imply "wait a minute" and continued to talk. While he waited, Eddie glanced at the photos on the wall. There was a picture of a policemen's ball from the seventies, a picture of an egg and spoon race with police officers and their children, and a third picture showed a charity dinner of police officers sitting with their biggest donors. Next to the Police Chief, sat Terry Palmer.

Brown answered questions with "yes" or "no." Eddie couldn't pick up any details, only Brown's agitation.

He tiptoed a few steps to a turn in the corridor and found a staffroom. Through the door's window, he saw police play pool and watch football on a large flatscreen TV. A small gold plaque on the door said, Staffroom renovation made possible by the generous donation of Terrance Palmer. "My thanks to the boys in blue, Terry."

"Oi," Brown said. "No walking off." He clicked his fingers and pointed at the floor near him, commanding Eddie like a dog.

"Understood." Brown hung up and looked Eddie up and down. "You're done."

Eddie gulped. "Pardon?"

"You're finished with the bathroom, yes?"

He nodded with his mouth open.

Brown and Eddie re-entered the interview room. Rex and the officer sat back laughing. Rex rolled his tongue while the officer wiggled his ears.

"But can you do this?" Rex's tongue touched his nose.

"I can't. You win. You're the bigger freak."

Rex laughed. "I told you. You can't out-freak me."

Brown banged his hands on the table. "Cut it out."

"Sorry boss. We've made progress. Rex here says he copied the documents proving their case."

"What?" Eddie said. "Why didn't you say?"

"You never asked."

"I asked if you backed it up."

Rex tsked. "You back up files. You copy paper. You can't back up paper."

Brown tensed up. "We best go get these papers of yours then."

ELEVEN

Rex and Eddie sat in the back of Brown's car as he drove towards their office. Eddie fidgeted as his brain mulled over the police station's connection with Terry Palmer. If Brown worked for Palmer, as Eddie believed, then they were in trouble.

Rex sat back and took in the ride. "A real police car. Amazing! Hey, why are these seats so uncomfortable?"

"They need to be a material that's easy to clean," Brown said. "So it won't absorb any liquids."

"What kind of liquids?" Rex said.

"Bodily fluids."

Eddie's nostrils flared at the idea.

Rex thought for a second. "What kind of bodily fluids?"

Brown set his gaze on Rex through the rear-view mirror. "All of them."

The pair sat forward with raised knees, so the least amount of them touched the seats' surface.

Eddie tapped a text message into his phone while he

kept one eye on Brown. He wrote, *I think he works for Palmer. Be careful.* Eddie pressed send.

Rex's phone beeped, but he was fixated on the police car's fixtures.

"So have you ever called for backup on your radio?"

"Yes," Brown said.

"Did you get a text?" Eddie asked.

"It's probably my sister asking about dinner for my nan."

"You gonna tell her you're busy?"

"Nah."

"What if it's not your nan?"

Rex scoffed. "No one else texts me but you and my sister. And you're right here. Why would you be texting me? That would be weird."

Eddie bared his teeth as Rex gazed outside and waved at the pedestrians. He smiled like he was being driven in a parade.

"Rex," Eddie whispered. He nodded his head at Rex's phone pocket. Rex read the message and frowned. He showed it to Eddie.

I think he words for prom we. Be careful.

Eddie wrote the message in such a panic, auto-correct butchered it. He tried to type again but his fingers involuntarily tapped all over the keypad. At least the first message contained actual words; this was complete gibberish.

Stupid nerves, he thought. *You're gonna get me killed.*

"Palmer," Eddie whispered while nodding at Brown. Rex blinked, not understanding the message. "Works for Palm—"

An emergency stop shoved Eddie's head into the back of the front seat.

Brown tutted. "Traffic."

Eddie shook it off and leaned his head against the door

window. About eight cars in front, he could see people and cars all gathered together.

The black SUV sped down the other side of the street. Eddie covered his face with his hand to hide from the driver.

Rex pointed out the window. "That's the car." Rex couldn't see Eddie shake his head. "Excuse me, Mister. That's the SUV that tried to kill us."

Brown's piercing eyes glared at them through the rear-view mirror. They stared back.

Loud sirens down the street broke the silence.

"Is there something the matter?" Eddie asked.

"I'll take a look." Brown stepped out. With a click of his key fob all the car doors locked.

"This isn't right."

"I know." Rex folded his arms. "He really should have offered for one of us to sit in the front seat."

"I mean he can't lock us in. We haven't been arrested. He works for Palmer."

"What makes you think that?"

The police radio crackled to life. "Fire at three six nine High Street." It was Brown's voice.

Eddie pushed his nose against the window, trying to get a look. "That's our office."

"I have the two arsonists in custody," Brown's voice said.

Rex looked to Eddie with genuine concern.

Eddie swallowed. "This is bad."

"I know, one of them's gonna get to sit in the front."

"We're the arsonists. They burnt our evidence, and now they're framing us for it."

"Should we call the police?"

Eddie narrowed his eyes. "I see a problem with that, don't you?"

"Oh, right."

Rex and Eddie pulled and pushed at the doors. The bulletproof glass was uncrackable. They rocked the car back and forth while screaming. Outside the car, their screams for help were a mild, dull tone. Their frantic actions made pedestrians avoid them more than anything.

Brown marched back to the car.

"Rex, stop it. We need to play dumb."

"How do we do that?"

"Just be normal." Eddie paused. "Or as normal as you can be."

Brown entered and buckled up.

"The street's blocked off. We best get back to the station and try again later."

The police radio crackled to life. "Understood D.I. Brown. Assistance will be ready for you at the station."

Brown leaned back in his seat and exhaled slowly. He flicked on the police lights and u-turned the vehicle. In the back window, Rex and Eddie watched their office burn.

"What's your endgame?" Eddie said.

Rex tapped his chin. "Buy a house, get a wife, maybe some kids."

"Not you. Brown."

"I'm just a D.I. in the line of duty."

"How'd Palmer find out?"

Brown gave a smug grin. "I don't understand the question."

"Well, you can lock us up, but we'll tell the truth. A judge will hear about this."

"Unless, you managed to distract me, and I crashed the car. Then you could escape," Brown said.

"Good idea." Rex raised an eyebrow. "So, um, what's your favourite colour?"

Brown swerved the car off the road and into another

vehicle. A big clunk, and the car rocked backwards and forwards.

"Hey Eddie, I did it."

"While I sit here unconscious you kick out the back window." He turned to the sorry pair and waited.

Eddie and Rex sat still, confused.

"Do it."

Rex laid on his back and kicked at the back window. It did nothing. He kicked again, nothing.

"This is really hard."

Brown pointed his gun at the back window through the steel mesh divider. "You might want to put your fingers in your ears." Rex and Eddie keenly did as they were told and squeezed up to their nearest door with anticipation.

The bullet fired a tiny hole into the reinforced glass. A few cracks spread out.

"Again," Brown said.

Rex kicked. Brown nodded toward Eddie. Both kicked away at the back window which remained in place.

"For goodness sake." Brown unlocked the doors. "I'll work out a story later. Now you escape."

"What's the catch?" Eddie said.

"Unable to apprehend the two escapees, I shoot them."

"Then why do we bother?"

"Because I'll definitely kill you if you stay."

"He's bluffing, Rex. If he was going to kill us why not just do it now?"

Brown cracked a smile. "More paperwork."

"I'm convinced." Rex opened the door and fled.

"Do I have time to take off my shoes?" Eddie said. "It's my first wear, and they're giving me blisters."

Brown pointed the gun at Eddie. "No."

"Fair enough." Eddie leapt out the car door and raced after Rex.

The pair ran down the street towards the burning office as Brown fired. They rushed towards a gang of football fans, all wearing the Cloisterham team colours and singing chants. Eddie accidentally bumped into one who shoved him against a wall.

"Watch where you're going, you ponce."

"Sorry, it's him. He was disrespecting us. Said anyone that supports Cloisterham is a sad act."

"Did he now?" the gang leader grumbled. The football fans backed away and set their sights on Brown. "Come on boys."

As Brown ran the football fans spread out and blocked the pavement.

The leader straightened his shoulders. "You got something to say about Cloisterham F.C?"

Brown pulled out his gun. "Get out of my way."

The football fans ran off in opposite directions. Rex and Eddie were gone.

The detective duo drank beer and shared a packet of crisps in a corner of The Jolly Codger, a small pub on the High Street with a funny smell. Its wobbly tables meant every inch had been covered by spilt beer at one point or another. The furniture was sticky, and the walls were damp.

Eddie curled his lip. "This is great."

"Really?"

"No, not really. We're on the run from gangsters and crooked coppers, we have no money, I bet our car was impounded again, we're framed fugitives, and I hate this pub."

"Why are we here then?"

"Because no one will look for us here. We don't know how long we were being followed. Maybe Stacey Lawrence's phone was tapped, and it has been since our first encounter. If that's the case, they've followed us to all our normal places."

"Like followed me home to my nan's?"

"Yes, your nan's."

"We've got to make sure she's okay."

"They're probably waiting outside your nan's for us to show up. She'll be safer with us in hiding. Only trouble is, this place closes at eleven. Then we need a new hiding spot."

"How about, we move to Scotland and keep our heads down."

"Why Scotland?"

"It's across the border. In movies, they always go to Mexico. Scotland is our Mexico."

"It's still in the UK."

"France?"

"Absolutely not. We'd be hated."

Rex hung his head low. "We don't seem to have many friends in England at the moment."

Eddie put his hand on Rex's shoulder. "Hey, we have each other." He sighed. "God, that's a miserable thought."

"We could go to Dublin, how many euros are there to a pound at the moment?"

"Last time I looked it was one and a quarter."

"How much money do we have?"

Eddie searched through his wallet. Nothing. He emptied his pockets. "One ten."

Rex perked up. "One hundred and ten."

"No. One pound, ten pence. We can't even get to Ireland."

"Ryan Air might have a deal. A pound could get one of us there."

"If by some chance they do, I can't search their website, because both our phones are out of credit." Eddie buried his head in his hand. "I'm a grown up. I should have a phone contract by now."

"It's okay Eddie, you can afford phone credit tomorrow, when Stacey gives you the five-grand. You can fly anywhere you want tomorrow."

"Are you joking? Stacey's hiding from Palmer. Going to her house is a complete waste of time."

"Okay, fine," Rex said. "You got any better ideas?"

TWELVE

Rex and Eddie weaved through the busy High Street crowd. The revellers were out for the pubs and clubs. The two detectives managed to walk unnoticed amongst the drunken singing, puking, and mild bouts of fisticuffs.

"Stacey's house is a bit of a walk," Eddie said. "A good ten miles at least."

Rex quickened his pace. "We're making a quick stop first to see Jim Jams."

Eddie stopped walking. "Not Jim Jams. Not after the day I've had."

"Why can't you two be friends?"

"He's a bad influence."

"I bet he's got a car. It's either Jim Jams, or we walk ten miles in the dark, in a town where the police are searching for us."

Eddie pursed his lips. "Fine. If you can find him."

Rex smiled. "He texted earlier to say he was working the door at The Queen Victoria pub."

The pair arrived outside the pub, a broad, cream

coloured building with black trim. Twenty people waited in line while Jim Jams, stood tall and proud, checked IDs at the door. He wasn't a classically good-looking man, with his prominent chin and flat nose, but his flair for fashion and friendly demeanour won people over.

"ID, ID, get your IDs out. Money at the ready," he called out.

Jim Jams multi-tasked by viewing drivers' licences, taking five-pound notes, and winking at the ladies. He caught Rex and Eddie out the corner of his eye.

"Fellas!"

Rex waved. "Hello, Jim Jams."

He beckoned the pair over. "What can I do you for? This place closes at midnight, but I'm headed to The Monte Carlo nightclub later if you're interested?"

"Nice," Rex said.

"We can't today."

Jim Jams continued to shuffle IDs and fivers while talking to them.

"Come on fellas, it's Friday night, what's the worst that could happen?"

"We could be framed for arson, and chased by a corrupt policeman, who works for a notorious gangster that wants us dead," Eddie said.

Jim Jams considered Eddie's words. "Granted, that's a possibility, but beer is buy one get one free from midnight to one. How pucker is that?"

"Jim Jams," Rex said. "Do you have a car?"

"Sort of."

"Oh good, can you give us a lift?"

"Yeah, no problem."

"Wait," Eddie said. "What does 'sort of' means?"

"It means I have access to a car. Or cars, plural."

Rex gave a nod. "Lovely."

Eddie folded his arms. "Explain."

"My mate Phil works at the impound. We take the cars out for a ride sometimes. I can give him a bell, see if we can borrow a car."

"A Morris Minor?" Eddie said.

"That's a bit specific, but I'll ask. Sure you don't have a better preference."

"Call your friend."

"Okay, let's do it." Jim Jams walked away from the door, leaving the line of confused punters awaiting entry.

Rex scratched his head. "What about your job?"

"Oh, this ain't a job. I'm a volunteer."

Eddie grimaced. "What does that mean?"

"Show up early enough, and everyone thinks you work there. I ask for ID and charge a fiver."

"You mean you're not collecting a cover charge?"

"Well, it covers my services."

"And the pub knows about it?"

"God no. Let's get going shall we." Jim Jams walked off with a quick, confident step. Rex and Eddie checked back at the line of people all patiently waiting. The pair shrugged it off and caught up with Jim Jams.

Thanks to Jim Jams, Rex and Eddie had the Morris Minor back and were headed towards Snodling. Jim Jams persuaded the pair to give him a ride to The Monte Carlo. The car pulled up outside the nightclub.

Eddie pulled the brake. "We're here."

Rex looked back and saw Jim Jams asleep. "He's taking a power nap."

"Wake him up."

"It's not possible. The man is a walking chemistry

experiment. You throw him off, and he'll be out of balance for days, maybe weeks. Besides, he's the heaviest sleeper I know."

"Fine, he'll have to come with us to Stacey's, and we'll drop him off when we come back."

The Morris Minor navigated down the dark country lane. Tim's gang had bashed in the headlights, before leaving Jim Jams borrowed two torches from the impound and taped them to the car's front. Although the lights helped, it was still hard with the lack of side mirrors and the fact that the passenger side windows had "wankers" sprayed over it.

"Eddie, do you think we should have taken a different car?"

"It's fine. We fixed the headlights. It'll just take a few more miles to air out the smell of urine."

"I mean, aren't we wanted by murderers and stuff? Aren't we sticking out?"

"I'm not stealing a car. Yes, there are gangsters and bent coppers after us, but I will not stoop to their level by stealing. I've got principles."

They pulled up outside Stacey's house and knocked on the door. There was no answer. They tried again. A third knock and a plump old lady opened the door. She repeatedly blinked as her eyes adjusted to the light.

"Yes, what is it?"

"We're looking for Stacey Lawrence," Eddie said. "We just have a few questions."

"There is no Stacey here. It's very late. Please leave."

"Do you know where she is? Did she leave any papers behind?"

"Please, I don't know a Stacey. You'll have to leave, or I'm calling the police."

"We get it. She's hiding. We're in the same boat."

The old lady slammed the door.

"Great, Brown will be here any second. We've got no leads, no proof, no money."

Rex smiled. "We've got a pound."

"What can we do with one pound?"

Rex and Eddie examined their options.

"We have the doctors and nurses," the Indian shopkeeper said. "There is a football one, and then there's the casino card for the playing of the fruit machine."

They stood over the shop counter examining the scratch card display.

"Shall we do the fruit machine?" Rex asked.

"The football one has a bigger prize," Eddie said.

Rex scowled. "I don't like football."

Eddie half-shrugged. "Me neither."

The shopkeeper leaned over the counter. "When you make up your mind, you tell me. In the meantime, step aside for the customers, thank you, please."

The pair shuffled to one side as a customer placed three bottles of vodka on the counter. It was Jim Jams.

"You're awake," Rex said.

"Yeah, I'm ready and raring to go. Shall we make our way to The Monte Carlo?"

"Did you lock up the car?" Eddie said.

Jim Jams wrinkled his nose. "Does it lock up?"

Eddie checked the shop window to make sure the battered up car was safe. The lights of one of the taped on torches flickered.

"I think you need new batteries for one of those flashlights. Allow me." Jim Jams grabbed a pack of batteries from the stand and placed them next to his vodka.

"What is that," Eddie asked, "your weekly shop?"

"It's for the weekend."

Eddie stared.

"I'm gonna share it," Jim Jams said.

The shopkeeper rang him up. "And some Absinth. And twenty fags, two packs. Oh, and a pack of skittles."

Jim Jams paid over two hundred pounds, which cleared him of his night's earnings.

"What's the upset, fellas?"

"We have one pound left to our names. We thought we'd buy a scratch card and skip the country with the winnings."

"Our friend won five grand and bought a new car," Rex said.

Eddie mugged. "I wouldn't call him a friend."

Jim Jams bagged up his alcohol and cigarettes. "Scratch cards? You want to be careful. Those things can be addictive."

"I think we'll be fine," Eddie said.

"Get the fruit machine one. It has the lowest odds."

Eddie checked the car. "It does?"

The shopkeeper nodded. "The man is right."

"We'll take the fruit machine scratch card please."

"Can I do the scratching, Eddie?" Rex snatched the card before Eddie could answer. "I think I should do it. I'm luckier. I won a school raffle once."

Eddie cocked his head. "Once?"

"Have you ever won a raffle?"

"Fine, go on then."

Rex did a little jump. "What do we scratch with?"

Eddie checked his pockets and turned to Jim Jams.

"Sorry fellas, I'm back to zero."

Eddie dug deep for the ten pence, his last coin, and handed it to Rex. Eddie read the instructions.

"According to the rules, we need three matching fruits on two lines to win a tenner. Three lines is five hundred. All four lines, and we win five thousand pounds."

The first line was a bust: two plums and a watermelon slice. The next two had matches, three apples on one, three watermelon slices on the second. They had won at least ten pounds. If they got the fourth line, they would win five hundred pounds.

Eddie grinned. "That's two plane tickets out of here."

Rex scratched the first box. It was a lemon. He took a deep breath and scratched the second box. It was also a lemon. He scratched the third box.

"What is it?" Eddie said.

Rex stared at the card.

The shopkeeper shook his fists. "Come on man. Tell us."

"It's a lemon," Rex said.

Jim Jams nodded. "Nice."

Eddie handed over the scratch card to the shopkeeper. "Five hundred pounds, please."

The shopkeeper slumped. "I can't give you the money."

A vein popped out of Eddie's neck "Why not?"

"Anything over two-fifty you have to send it to the lottery commission. They'll give you the money in two to three weeks."

"What?" Eddie threw his hands in the air. "We could be dead in two to three weeks."

"That's true for all of us," Jim Jams said. "It's all temporary."

"Beautiful," Rex said.

"Yes, thank you, Jim Jams. But that's not very helpful."

Eddie waved the ticket at the shopkeeper. "How much would you buy it for?"

"Me? I can't play. I'm a trader. If I won, it would be invalid."

"Jim Jams?"

"I'll give you vodka and the skittles?"

Eddie clenched his teeth. "So if we won a tenner, we'd have a tenner right now."

"Yes."

"Kingdom for a horse," Jim Jams said with a smile.

Eddie threw his hands up. "What am I supposed to do now? Wander the streets waving down black SUVs until one shoots me in the face?"

Rex's face contorted. "I think that's the opposite of what we want to do."

Eddie pointed at Rex. "This is your fault."

Jim Jams raised his palms. "Easy there Eddie, Rex is doing his best."

"How is it my fault?" Rex asked.

"You convinced me to do this. To invest my money, to rent a murder scene, you found the reward, chasing it with you is what got me into this mess. Why do I listen to you? Why am I friends with you?"

"That's harsh," Jim Jams said.

"It sounds like he has a point," the shopkeeper said.

"No, *this* is harsh. The only reason to stay anywhere near you right now is because I only have a fifty percent chance of getting shot when there are two targets."

Rex stood frozen.

"What have you got to say for yourself?" Eddie said.

"Lemon?" Rex mumbled.

"Oh, shut up."

"Hey, you asked him to talk," Jim Jams said. "Now fair enough, it wasn't the best answer."

"No. Lemon!" Rex's eyes widened. "She didn't know where the lemons were."

"What are you talking about?"

"Stacey, she said she didn't have any lemons."

Eddie screwed up his face. "Right?"

"She didn't know where anything was."

"That *was* odd," Eddie said. "She didn't know her way around her own kitchen?"

Rex grabbed Eddie's shoulder. "It wasn't her kitchen. Stacey Lawrence doesn't live there."

"She doesn't live there," they both said, jumping up and down.

Jim Jams and the shopkeeper looked at each other with confusion.

"Harold said she never visited Derek at the office. Not once," Eddie said.

"He didn't even see her at Christmas."

Eddie stopped jumping. "Why would you put up a reward for someone you didn't like? A father you don't even see at Christmas? Did she set us up?"

Rex stopped too. "She's a bad person."

"She is a bad person." Eddie agreed. "We've got to speak to that old lady again."

THIRTEEN

Eddie pressed the doorbell to Stacey Lawrence's so-called house. Rex and Jim Jams stood behind him with folded arms, ready to intimidate. The old lady opened the door a crack.

"I'm calling the police." She pushed the door closed.

Eddie jammed his foot in. The door sprang back open as Eddie screamed in agony.

Eddie hobbled in a circle. "That really hurt."

The old lady huffed at him. "Well, you shouldn't put your foot in there."

"She's got a point," Rex added.

"Please, we know Stacey Lawrence doesn't live here. But she was here this morning. She invited us."

"That's not possible."

"Who was here? Did you let anyone in?"

"You've got the wrong house. My house had a film crew here."

"A film crew?" Eddie asked.

"A film producer rented the house last week. They came today for a re-shoot."

"And you were here too?"

"They put me up in a fancy hotel. Oh, it was nice, delicious scones."

Jim Jams stepped forward. "Madam, we're from the film crew."

"You are?"

"Yes!" He steps forward, big and tall. "And I'm the director."

"Oh yes, well you look very artsy."

"Ah, you have a keen eye. You'd be good as a casting director."

"I would?"

"Indeed, have you ever worked in the theatre, my dear?"

"I haven't, no."

"Never done a play?"

"Well, I was in the choir for a church nativity play."

"And I'm sure even the great north star looked dim next to you."

She blushed. "Oh my."

"Now my dear, this man," he pointed at Eddie, "is my prop master, and unfortunately he's quite the incompetent."

"Excuse me?" Eddie said.

"I'll hear no more of it, Eddie. You are forgiven."

Eddie crossed his arms tight.

Jim Jams put his arm around the old lady. "My colleague here left some important props behind. Some papers. It's crucial that we retrieve them for tomorrow's shoot. Have you seen any letters or other papers?"

"I haven't, no."

"May we come in and find them? Otherwise, I'll be forced to fire this idiot monkey man."

Eddie wanted to strangle Jim Jams but swallowed his pride.

"I have a wife and child," Eddie added. "Or did, depends how the night goes."

She nodded. "You best come in."

Inside, the three checked every surface for the evidence. The old lady brought in a tray of tea.

"I must say, it is odd to hear that name, Stacey Lawrence. That's the name of the lady that used to live here."

All three stopped searching and turned to the old lady.

"Do you know her?" Rex said. "Blonde hair, early thirties."

"Oh no. She'd be in her forties now. She had brown hair. I've got a picture somewhere; she sent me a photo when she got settled."

Eddie's eyebrows lowered. "Settled?"

"Yes, she emigrated to Australia."

Eddie, Rex, and Jim Jams huddled together.

"We were hired by an impostor. She's in Australia, that's why she never visited his office," Eddie said.

The old lady brought out the photo of Stacey Lawrence. She was a middle-aged, stout brunette, with a bulbous nose just like her father.

Rex scratched his head. "But if Stacey Lawrence is in Australia, who hired us?"

"And why did she hire us? Or pick this house?" Eddie turned to the old woman. "Did the producer leave any contact info?"

"No, I'm afraid not. They just came, paid in cash and left. He was a lovely man. Tall, a bit boney. Pale face."

"Brown," Eddie said.

"No, I said pale."

Eddie turned to Rex. "Brown was the producer. He orchestrated the whole thing."

"And he still found time to shoot a film," Rex said.

Eddie pulled Rex aside, and Jim Jams followed.

"The film is a cover. The real question is, why did they pick the real Stacey Lawrence's house?"

"The property sales website," Rex said. "I checked to see if she was the owner of the house. I saw her name on the free access page, but I didn't pay to get sales dates."

Eddie raised his eyebrows. "You researched the property?"

"To see if the house was in Derek's name. She might have killed him for the inheritance and put up a reward to look innocent. You know, in case she was our first femme fatale."

"They picked Stacey Lawrence's house so it would be traced back to her. Because they thought a real detective would check the property deeds."

Rex grinned. "I did real detective work?"

"Yeah, you're a real detective." Eddie patted Rex on the shoulder. "You used careful data recollection which led us to—"

"Nothing," Jim Jams said. "The only reason you've come this far is because of Rex. Inside that twisted noggin of his, is the ability to smile in the face of death, until he sees something smile back at him. Even if what smiled back was a useless scratch card."

Eddie sighed. "He's right. We made it this far because you worked out Stacey was a fake."

"Now, I couldn't have done that if you didn't sort out all the other stuff. You're good at worrying for me. Papers and receipts and backups. We found the evidence because you did the data collecting."

Jim Jams waves his finger between the pair. "Where

does that leave you two now?"

Eddie drew a blank. "We're at a dead end."

"Well, that's pucker. You fellas wanna go to The Monte Carlo?"

"We need to do research," Eddie said. "We can drop you off."

Rex scratched his head. "Where are we gonna research? We're homeless."

Eddie thought about it for a second. He looked to Jim Jams. "Sorry fellas, I still don't know where I shall hang my hat tonight."

"What do you do to go on the Internet?" Eddie said.

"Nothing, if I want to see a cat do cute things. I'd visit a friend with a cat."

Eddie snapped his fingers. "The library."

Rex turned to the old lady as they headed to the door. "Oh, just one more thing."

"What's that dear?"

Eddie opened the door. "If you ask her where she was on the night of October twenty-eighth, so help me."

"I just wanted to ask if I could use the bathroom."

Eddie drove the Morris Minor into town while Rex helped Jim Jams create a cocktail out of vodka, orange juice, wine and five-hour-energy. He didn't have a glass, so he swirled the ingredients in his mouth and swallowed.

"Are you sure you boys don't want some?"

Rex and Eddie shook their heads.

"It'll keep you going until at least five a.m."

"Thanks all the same," Eddie said.

They dropped him off outside The Monte Carlo and continued into town. Rex's seat buzzed and beeped.

"Um, Eddie. My seat is being weird."

"What do you mean weird?"

"It's buzzing and beeping. Do car bombs buzz and beep?"

"Why would you say that?"

Rex tensed his neck muscles. "We left the car at the police station. Brown might have messed with it."

Eddie's breath quickened. "I'll pull over."

"What if that's what triggers it?"

"Oh crap, I don't know. Can you look under?"

"What if it's weight sensitive? What if I move and set it off?"

"Okay, let's think about this. We don't know what triggers it. So how about we look it up on my phone."

"Where's your phone?"

In a panic, Eddie's brain struggled to recall. "Uh, it's under your seat."

"Now what do we do?"

Eddie calmed. "Rex, the buzzing and beeping is my phone."

"Oh." Rex shoved his hand under the seat and reached for it.

"You have a missed call from Melinda."

"Ah crap, I'm meant to take her out tonight."

Eddie sped up and drove to her flat. Outside Melinda's building, he pushed the entryway's buzzer.

Rex sulked. "I wanted to push the button."

Eddie lowered to a whisper. "Don't say a word, Rex. You are not here."

The intercom crackled. "Hello?"

"Hi Melinda, it's Eddie."

"I'll be right down."

"Actually, can we come up for a minute?"

"We?"

"Me, the uh, the royal we, needs a wee."

"Okay."

The door buzzed, and the lock released. Rex and Eddie jogged up the stairs to Melinda's door. Eddie pushed Rex against the wall and knocked.

"You hide here until I've explained the situation."

Melinda opened the door in a sparkly dress and wavy hair.

"Come on in."

Eddie smiled wide. "You look nice."

"Thanks, these are my special going out clothes."

"Yeah, about that. Maybe we could stay in."

Melinda folded her arms. "I thought we were going to celebrate your big case."

"Um, yeah. I'm a bit tired. Maybe we could snuggle up and watch a movie. Go out another night."

Melinda's shoulders slumped. "You haven't changed at all. You're still the boring boy who's going nowhere."

"It's not like that."

"I'm not interested, Eddie. I want you to leave."

"We'll still do a surprise night out, just not tonight."

"You always want to stay in or do the same things. I want excitement and adventure. I want to be surprised."

He plastered a smile on his face. "Rex is outside."

She glared at him. "Why are you telling me that?"

"Surprise?"

Melinda crossed her arms. "No."

"So I'm getting kicked out because I'm boring and have no adventures?"

"Yes."

"Well, then. It may please you to know, I am actually a fugitive from the law after being framed for arson. The case I solved was murder, and the murderer is a big-time gangster who sent an assassin to kill me and Rex."

"Really?" she said with sarcasm.

Eddie gave a short, sharp nod. "Really."

"Really?" she said, sincere this time.

"Yeah, so don't think of it as a boring night in. But a dangerous safe house hiding two heroes while they fend off gangsters, police, and snipers."

Melinda's eyes when round. "Snipers?"

"Yeah."

"You should leave."

"But I thought this is what you wanted?" Eddie said with genuine confusion.

"I want you out." Melinda pushed Eddie towards the door and shoved him out. Rex hid at the side of Melinda's door.

"But I did it all for you."

She slammed the door. Eddie slumped.

Rex smiled. "So, how'd it go?"

"Hello, we're here to visit Billy," Eddie told the nurse.

"Billy who?"

"Uh, Billy Quid?"

"I've got a William Bishop?"

Eddie winced. "No other Billys?"

"No."

"William Bishop it is then."

"Room eighty-two. Visitor hours close in ten minutes."

Rex and Eddie headed down the corridor while keeping an eye open for potential assassins.

"Hey Eddie, if we do get shot, at least we're close to the Accident & Emergency room. Right?"

"Please, Rex. Not now."

The pair entered room eighty-two, a square room with

six beds partitioned by blue curtains. Rex and Eddie popped their heads in a few curtains until they found Billy asleep with his arm in a sling.

"Sorry, Billy," Eddie said.

In the distance, they could hear a nurse order visitors to leave. Next to Billy, they saw a spare bed. Both had the same thought. They drew the dividing curtain and laid down.

"Hey Eddie, do you want to be the big spoon or the little spoon."

"I want to be two equal spoons laying next to each other."

The nurse switched off the lights, and they lay in the dark.

"Hey, Eddie. Good work today."

"You too. Good night."

Rex's stomach grumbled. "I'm hungry."

"We'll see if we can share Billy's breakfast in the morning. He'll probably still be sleeping."

"What do you want to do tomorrow?"

"We're gonna go to the library as soon as it opens and search for Stacey."

"Real detective work?"

"Real detective work," Eddie said with a yawn. "You were right; she is our first femme fatale."

"Hey, Eddie."

"Please, Rex. I'm exhausted."

"Sorry, it's just. I don't remember the last time we had a sleepover."

"Yeah, it's been a while. If you're quiet, I promise we can have another one soon. Maybe go camping."

"Deal. Good night, Eddie."

"Good night, Rex."

FOURTEEN

Outside the library, Rex and Eddie shivered. Rex's blazer gave him an extra layer, but Eddie struggled in just a collared shirt. He made a vow to himself, from this day forward he would keep a jacket on hand in case of future assassination attempts.

When the doors opened, Rex rushed to the nearest computer. The sign said fifteen minutes per person. They found the Snodling house on property websites. Using a free fourteen-day trial, they searched previous house owners to confirm Stacey Lawrence sold it ten years ago.

Using a careers website, they found her CV showing she currently worked as a hospital administrator in Perth, Australia.

"How do we find the girl we met?" Eddie asked. "All I remember was that she was late twenties, blonde shoulder length hair, and she made a terrible cup of tea."

"Was it shoulder length?" Rex said. "I thought it was just below her ears. I remember she had blue eyes, no wait, green."

"This is useless. How are we detectives if we can't even remember what she looked like?"

Rex rubbed his chin. "I think they were blue."

"There's no way of finding her with so little information."

"The Equity website. It's all the union actors. If we do a casting search, we can find her."

Eddie bobbed his head. "If she's an actress."

Rex typed in her physical description and age range on the Equity site. The site brought up over two thousand searches. Rex scrolled through each headshot one by one looking for Stacey. When Rex's fifteen-minute allotment was over, they were only seven hundred deep. The computer screen counted down and flashed red. Rex attempted to bash the keys, but it did not respond.

"You'll have to stop now," said the spindly librarian from her desk. Her bun of dark and grey hair created a purple orb above her head. She walked over in a deliberate manner, as if she balanced the purple ball on top of her skull.

"We just need a few more minutes."

"It's fifteen minutes per library member."

"I'm a member," Eddie said.

He typed his library card number and pressed enter. A pop up read, *There is an issue with your account. Please see the librarian.* Eddie dashed to the counter, but the old librarian took her time joining him. He tapped his hand on the tabletop.

She looked at him over her glasses. "You have an outstanding fine. Five pounds."

Eddie frowned. "I don't have any money."

"Well, I'm sorry, once fines reach five pounds the account is locked."

"So anything below five pounds is fine?"

"Yes."

"Rex, do you still have the ten pence?"

Rex pulled the tiny silver coin from his pocket and bolted to the counter.

"No running," the librarian said.

"Sorry."

Rex handed over the ten pence coin. She typed the information.

"Your account is now active."

The pair ran towards the computer station.

"No running."

They speed-walked the rest of the way.

The extra fifteen minutes of computer time did not prove fruitful. With five minutes to go, they had another four hundred actresses to view.

"She's not here, Rex."

"We can narrow it down. Did you see the ballet shoes, the ones I tripped on? Maybe they were hers."

Eddie added ballet into the search form. Two hundred results.

Rex shuffled in his seat, excited. "She was good at throwing fruit. Good aim."

"There isn't a fruit-throwing option."

"Give athletic a try."

The new search brought up sixty results. They raced through each one and finished with two minutes to spare. She wasn't there.

"It's over."

Rex shrugged. "Oh well, it was worth a try."

"How can you be this relaxed? You really do smile death in the face. You have to do something. Some weird leap in logic. We have to find the lying cow or we're dead." Eddie paused. "Lying cow," he repeated.

"Okay, Eddie. Calm down."

"Don't you get it. Lying cow!"

"Shh," said the librarian at her desk.

"Sorry," Eddie lowered to a whisper. "She lies." He changed the age category to young twenties. Thirty searches. The fifteenth profile was her.

Eddie hissed. "Becky Cooper."

"That headshot doesn't do her justice. I mean she was much prettier in person, and it doesn't give off the smoky lying femme-fatale casting."

"Yes, thank you, Rex. Can we focus?"

They searched her name on Facebook, but the account was private. Twitter showed a bunch of Becky Coopers until the computer screen lit up with a red flash.

The librarian stood over them. "Time's up."

"Just a few more minutes please."

"I'm sorry, but it's fifteen minutes per person."

"In a few more minutes we'll be done."

She rested her hands on her hips. "Yes, well, everyone thinks they're a special case."

Rex stood up. "It's an emergency, lady."

"An emergency on your part does not constitute an emergency on my part."

"Please, will you give us more time?" Eddie said.

"Absolutely not. I must make everything available to all customers. I can't have you hold up other people."

"Who are we holding up?" Eddie raised his hands and twirled. "There is no one else on the computers."

The librarian pushed her glasses up her nose. "It's policy."

Rex, snuck away to the librarian's counter as Eddie argued with the librarian.

"Fine," Eddie barked, "the library is stupid anyway."

"Very well," the librarian said. "Be on your way."

At her computer, Rex searched for Becky Cooper on Twitter.

"This library card is useless. I'm gonna tear it up." Eddie attempted to rip the laminated card but merely bent it at best. "I'm gonna rip it to pieces." He tried again but didn't leave a mark. The Librarian folded her arms, tired of Eddie's little fit.

Rex gave Eddie a thumbs up. He was impressed Eddie managed to drag the performance out, unaware Eddie genuinely tried to rip it.

"When I get home, I'm gonna cut it up with scissors. So there."

Rex read a tweet from @Becky85 about a ballet audition.

"Yes!" Rex threw his hands up in celebration. The Librarian turned to her desk.

"You can't be back there," she said.

Panicked, Rex tapped the print button. Across the desk, the printer fed out a page.

"Printouts are twenty pence each," she said as she marched over.

She reached for the paper tray, but Rex snatched the document. The librarian cornered him.

"Rex, throw it."

"No throwing allowed."

Rex chucked the paper, but it looped in the air and floated back to him. He made a paper plane with precision and focus while batting away the angry librarian with his kicking leg.

Eddie waved his arms. "Just throw it as a ball."

Rex screwed it up and chucked it at Eddie. The librarian made a dive for the printout, but Eddie shoved one hand in her face and grabbed the paper ball. The pair ran and didn't stop until the library was a pinprick in their view.

Eddie unwrapped the ball of paper. "What is it?"

"Tweets by Becky Cooper," Rex said, still catching his breath.

Eddie read through the tweets.

@Becky85 Open mic at the Spout 'n' Bottle tonight. Come on by.

@Becky85 Don't forget it's Drum and Bass at The Spout tonight. I'll be serving.

@Becky85 Booked my holiday to Jamaica, Well proud. #ActingJob.

@Becky85 Free sandwiches and doughnuts at noon every weekday @thespoutnbottle.

"I bet we're the acting job," Eddie said. "She was hired to set us up. But why?"

Rex pointed at the printed tweet. "To go to Jamaica?"

"No, why was she hired? It was either Palmer, or Brown working for Palmer, but why put out a ransom for a murder you committed?"

"Maybe Stacey, I mean Becky, knows."

"Let's go to The Spout 'n' Bottle and talk to her."

Rex grinned. "And eat doughnuts?"

"That's not the primary purpose."

"But if they're there?"

Eddie half-nodded. "Then it would be rude not to eat at least one doughnut."

FIFTEEN

"We're gonna need beer money," Rex said as Eddie drove.

"I spent our last ten pence. Want to call Jim Jams?"

"Mid-mornings are his extended nap times. What about a loan?"

"The bank doesn't really do beer money loans."

"Why not, it's just a few quid?"

They both had the same idea. "Billy!"

Rex and Eddie sneaked into Billy's hospital room. He was asleep, and they wanted to keep it that way.

"Aren't we stealing by not asking?" Rex whispered.

"We don't have time."

"But what about our principles?"

"He always borrows money. He'd be fine with it. If he was awake, I'd explain it to him."

Eddie grabbed the small bag of pound coins. The heaviness surprised him. As they tiptoed out, Rex knocked over a metal table, which awoke Billy.

He rolled side to side in his bed. "What's happening?"

"Shhh. Go to sleep," Eddie said. The coins jiggled as they ran out.

"Me pounds!" Billy called out.

The Spout 'n' Bottle was a pub and club between East Cloisterham train station and the High Street. It used to be an old jeans factory, and its industrial atmosphere was a hit with the Emo crowd. Steel beams paired up with hanging chains and gothic murals that mixed skulls and drug culture with the odd image of historical places.

The building's three floors featured band stages, pool rooms, beer gardens, DJ dance rooms, and several bars. During the day only the front bar was open, which made it easy to find Becky Cooper.

Rex and Eddie approached the bar. Becky, in the uniform black top and fluffed up hair, served another patron. She was in a much lighter mood when not playing the grieving daughter.

"This is it, Rex. Brace yourself … Rex?"

Rex helped himself to the doughnut tray.

"Rex come here. Here. Now."

"What can I get you?" Becky asked, not identifying them in the poor light.

"Two beers, please."

She recognised the voice and went rigid. "What do you two want?"

"Thwoo bhears," Rex said with a mouthful of doughnut.

"Everything all right?" the barman asked her.

"Yeah, fine." She poured their drinks.

Eddie leaned closer. "Where are the documents?"

"I gave them to the man."

"You best start from the beginning?"

"Yeah, we want every detail," Rex said, between bites of doughnut. He built a tower out of the remaining ones, perfectly balanced on a single napkin. "Don't leave any details out."

"Why should I help you?"

"Because you're gonna get us killed."

"And?"

"And?" Eddie said. "It's not fair."

"If I help you, you've got to protect me, yeah?"

"You want us to protect you?"

Eddie's lack of confidence caused Becky to step back. She reassessed the pair. Eddie scratched his head while Rex gorged on doughnuts.

"No one else has offered, so yeah."

"We'll do our best," Eddie said. "As long as the information is good. We want details."

"One of the bouncers here, he said he knew someone that needed an actor. I'm an actor really, this is a day job. I'm between agents at the moments but—"

"Maybe not all the details," Eddie said.

"They needed someone to pretend for them. It was just meant to be over the phone. They gave me a mobile and said if it rang I was meant to say I'm Stacey Lawrence and offer five grand for information on the death of my father. I took the phone. They paid me a hundred quid a week to keep it on me. It never rang. They told me to keep a hold of it."

"Terry Palmer?" Eddie said.

Rex choked a little on his food.

Becky quietened to a whisper. "I never met Terry Palmer, but I'm sure they work for him."

"Why?"

"Because they were upset when you linked the murder to him."

"What happened after the phone?"

"No one called it. After two months they told me to give it back. I took the money, and it was over with. Then last week they came here and told me there was a message on the phone, and I had to return the call." She pointed at Rex. "The message was from him."

"So they wanted to make sure they tied all their loose ends," Eddie said. "Find out if anyone could link Palmer to Lawrence's death."

"I called you back and arranged the meeting like they asked. A tall man with a blue raincoat and a gun listened in as you talked."

Eddie nodded. "That's probably our detective friend."

"When I kicked you out—"

"The fruiting."

"Sorry, it was a stressful day. I thought if I got rid of you fast, life would go back to normal."

"But?"

"They came back with the phone. They thought, if you two idiots—"

"Hey," Rex said.

"Their words, not mine. If you two found anything, then Palmer could still go down for murder."

Eddie narrowed his eyes. "So you called us and spent the money on a trip to Jamaica?"

"No one expected you to find anything."

"Did you see what happened to the evidence?"

"The tall man. He listened in the other room. When you left he burned the papers in front of me."

"So then they followed us?"

"Yes."

"Did they follow us before that?"

"No. It was just the tall man the first time."

"Your nan's safe, Rex."

Rex smiled, revealing doughnut clumps between his teeth.

"Who's the bouncer that got you the job?"

"Louie Burton, but he died a few months ago. He was found in the river. His belly was full of holes."

"He was shot?" Rex said.

"He was stabbed with a sword."

Becky covered her face. Her eyes welled up. "I think Louie killed your man, and he was a loose end. Now there are three loose ends left. You, him, and me."

Eddie furrowed his brow. "They paid you off."

"I don't think that matters to them. They're paranoid enough to put out a reward for their own killing. It's all a bit much, isn't it?"

"Would you be a witness to the documents? Corroborate our story in court?"

"I wouldn't make it to the court date."

"Then we can't help you."

"Witnesses can be killed, and we will be killed," she said. "But we can mail your backup of the documents to every newspaper in the country. Then killing us does nothing, there'd be no point."

Rex and Eddie stared at their feet.

"We don't have our backup anymore," Eddie admitted.

"What? What kind of idiot loses … forget it. Well, that's great. You've got nothing else in the office?"

"The tall man had it set on fire."

"He blamed us," Rex said. "What a cheek."

Eddie's brows knitted. "Did you ever see a black SUV? Do you know the driver?"

Her eyes widened. "The man with the Glasgow Smile?"

"Happy Scottish people?" Rex said.

"It's when they cut both your cheeks." She mimed her cheeks being cut. "To give you two scars up the sides of your face."

"That's disgusting," Rex said. "That's enough to put a man off his food." He licked his sugar-coated fingers.

"Great, so we have a gangster, a bent policeman, and a scarred assassin after us."

Rex grinned. "It's like we're James Bond."

"Except we're stuck in Cloisterham, gadget-less, we've no experience, and instead of a martini, we've got a flat beer with too much head."

"Hey," Becky said.

"No offence."

"It is a bit flat." Rex nodded. "But the doughnuts are good. Who made them?"

"It's a Tesco's value pack."

"We should get these next time we stake out, eh Eddie? Good snack food."

Eddie tapped his forehead. "We need to follow our footsteps. Somewhere, there's a connection."

"Laing," Rex said and bit into a cheese roll. Eddie hated it when Rex jumped from dessert to a savoury meal, but that was an argument for a different time.

"John Laing has nothing to do with it."

Rex raised a finger. "He said Lawrence stole stories. Palmer killed his brother in the seventies, so Lawrence sat on that story for decades. Maybe he pitched it to Laing for Taskforce?" He bit into the cheese roll. "There must be older documents."

Eddie's back straightened. "That's genius."

Rex bit his sandwich. "Oh, it's nothing. People get too full for dessert, but not me. I eat the doughnuts first and then fill up on the meal—"

"I mean Laing. Not the cheese roll, that's disgusting."

Becky placed her hands on her hips. "I made those."

"Not the cheese roll itself, eating it after a doughnut. We're off track. Rex, we need to see Laing."

"I'm coming with you," Becky said.

"Why?"

"Because, I don't want you to screw it up."

Rex and Eddie assessed her answer and nodded in agreement.

Rex, Eddie, and Becky approached Laing's front door. Each of them waited for the other to press the doorbell.

"You ring it," Eddie said.

"No, you," Rex said.

"He likes you."

"It's your turn."

"How is it my turn?"

Becky rolled her eyes and pressed the doorbell. Laing opened the door.

He sneered. "Didn't expect to see you two again."

Eddie smiled. "I know, we left in a hurry, but—"

"Come to pay your tab?"

"Uh, sure?" Eddie studied Laing's face to see if that was the right answer. Laing didn't respond. "How, uh, how much was it?"

"Forty-two in total."

"Oh, right, well, we have—" Eddie counted up the bag of pound coins they borrowed from Billy. "Twenty-eight pounds."

"Forget it. You can't put a price on knowing where you stand with people."

"Sorry, we had an emergency," Rex said. "We didn't

mean to skip out on the tab. Plus, you look like you can afford it."

Laing crossed his arms. "What's that supposed to mean?"

Eddie stepped forward. "What Rex means is you have a lovely nice house, you've got your own company. Forty-two quid probably isn't a big deal compared to your elaborate fountain in the backyard."

"How do you know about my fountain?"

"Well, I uh?"

"You've been nosing around my property?"

"No."

Laing's dog scampered to the front door with Eddie's old shoe in its mouth. The dog nudged it at Eddie's hand.

Eddie took the shoe to calm the dog. "That's weird, eh?"

"Goodbye, gentleman." Laing pushed the door closed.

"Please, we just have a question. One question."

Eddie's foot blocked the closing door.

"Ouch, why do I think that's gonna work."

"Please," Rex said. "Did Lawrence ever talk to you about Terry Palmer? Or tell a story about a gangster throwing blood-soaked clothes in the river?"

Laing opened the door a little.

"Terry Palmer is trying to kill us," Eddie said. "If Lawrence said anything about Palmer's crime, you can save our lives."

Laing stroked his beard in shock.

Eddie pointed at Becky. "And hers."

Becky raised a hand. "Hi."

"No, but I hope it works out." A smiled grew on Laing's face. "I hope you do clear your name and lock up the bad men after you. I hope you survive this whole ordeal."

"Really?" Eddie said, touched by the gesture.

Rex beamed. "That's nice."

"Yeah, I hope you survive it all and then get cancer." Rex and Eddie's warm and fuzzy feelings vacated fast. "And then I hope your cancer gets cancer. I don't want to see you on my doorstep ever again." Laing slammed the door shut.

The three took in what just happened.

Rex raised a hand. "Is that because he wants the cancer to kill the cancer, and we become healthy? Or, did he wish us a double dose of cancer?"

"He meant double cancer," Eddie said.

Becky headed to the car. She turned to face the pair. "So does this whole Columbo act normally work for you?"

Rex and Eddie pulled confused faces.

"You know, you act stupid so they drop their defences, and then you strike."

Eddie shook his head. "It's not an act."

The three walked up the path to the battered Morris Minor.

"Now, what?" Becky said.

Rex and Eddie got in the car. Becky stomped behind them. Eddie sat at the steering wheel.

Becky knocked Eddie's headrest. "Hello? Now what?"

"Nothing, Laing was the last option. Even if he did remember Lawrence's story, he left all the TV stuff behind when Taskforce ended."

Rex hit the dashboard. "He left it all at the old TV studio."

Eddie's jaw dropped. "We can search for an early draft of Lawrence's ideas and link Palmer to the murder. We need to go back to the old TV studio."

Eddie started the car.

SIXTEEN

"Three for laser tag please."

The beehived lady rang up the cash register. "That will be forty-five quid."

Eddie splashed their stash of pound coins on the counter.

The beehive lady counted them up. "That's twenty-eight."

Rex and Eddie turned to Becky. She rolled her eyes and forked over the rest of the money.

"Shouldn't we get another ticket?" Rex said.

"Why?" Eddie said.

"Because I called backup?"

Becky sighed relief. "You guys have backup?"

Eddie's face scrunched up. "We have backup?"

"Yeah, well, I texted Jim Jams."

Eddie turned to Becky. "We don't have backup."

"The blues are already in," the beehive lady said. "You can go put on your body packs and guns. Three against three."

In the weapons chamber, Eddie poked at his body pack's faulty wires. He hoped to stop the electrocutions but gave himself a shock instead.

"Rex, please don't get too excited this time. Our job is to get to the office. Not shoot at children."

"What if they shoot first?"

"No."

Rex pouted and looked away.

"You hear me, Rex?"

The voice recording began: "Battle commences in three, two, one." The door slid open and smoke blew in their faces. Rex, Eddie, and Becky dashed through the smoke-filled arena. As they sprinted towards the fire exit, they passed several neon lights creating a pulsing effect as the pair whooshed by. At the door, a six-foot-five man wearing the blue pack stepped in front of them.

"Excuse me," Eddie said. "We aren't really here to play."

He lifted his head, and the blue UV light lit his face. He had scar lines from ear to ear. It was the Glasgow Smile, and his gun was real. "Neither am I."

Eddie swallowed. Knowing Rex would freeze in a panic, Eddie awaited a quick death.

Rex fired his laser gun at the Glasgow Smile's chest. An electric shock sparked through the man's chest. He buzzed for a few seconds and dropped his gun. Eddie snatched up the weapon while Rex fired his laser a second time. The Glasgow Smile fell to his knees.

"Do something," Becky said.

Eddie lifted the gun and hit the assassin in the head with the handle. The Glasgow Smile took the hit and scowled at Eddie. Giving the man's head a second whack, Eddie accidentally squeezed the trigger. The assassin dropped to the floor as the fired bullet took out a light fixture. A spotlight above flared, and sparks rained down. Eddie couldn't hear the light pop as his ears rang from the gun firing.

"Crap," Eddie said. "I think we gave away our position."

"We?" Becky said.

The grated floor above rattled and shook as the other two killers trotted towards them.

"They're on the second floor," Eddie said.

Eddie, Rex, and Becky burst through the fire exit into the hallway. They rushed to the next fire exit door, Eddie's shoes rubbed at his blisters with each step. Rex opened the fire door half a foot before it smacked against something. Outside, the black SUV blocked their path.

Eddie looked back at the arena fire door. "The only way out is through the battle zone."

Becky's jaw dropped. "I'm not going back out there."

Rex shrugged. "We may as well get what we came for then."

He ran up the stairs and kicked the office door. His foot bounced back and left an awful twinge in his reverberating knee.

Eddie and Becky followed.

"Let me try." Eddie gave the door a few kicks but tired quickly.

"What's wrong with you?" Becky said.

Eddie crouched down. "It's solid wood."

"Wood is hard," Rex said.

"Just use your head."

Rex grimaced. "Won't that hurt too?"

"Yeah, that sounds painful."

"No, I mean think about it. The gun?"

Eddie held out the gun, scrunched up his face, and put

his spare finger in one of his ears. Becky and Rex stood back.

Bang! Eddie's hands flung back from the pressure of the gun.

All three opened their eyes and saw a perfect round hole an inch below the handle.

"Now what?" Rex said.

Rex and Eddie rammed the door in unison. The door opened with a forceful crack. The office was empty, no furniture, not a single piece of paper; all the potential evidence was gone.

Eddie's whole body went slack.

Rex's eyebrows raised. "Wow, they've cleaned up in here."

"Sorry boys." Becky grabbed the gun from his hand and pointed the weapon at Rex and Eddie.

Eddie raised his hands. "Perfect."

"Put your hands up, Rex," she said.

Rex pointed his laser gun at her.

"Rex, do what she says." He didn't budge.

Becky waved the gun at him. "Put your hands up, you idiot."

"Rex, we've been beat."

Rex's eyes shifted between Eddie and Becky. His hands clutched his plastic laser gun.

"Where'd the papers go?" Eddie asked.

"Laser Flux is under new management," Becky said.

"Palmer?" he asked.

She nodded.

"You think this will make you safe? That they won't kill you."

"I've shown my loyalty."

"And what loyalty has Palmer shown you?"

A second of doubt distracted her and Rex fired his

laser. Her body pack's LED lights lit up as she received an electric spark. She held the gun tight and re-aimed on them. Rex fired again. The laser's cheap whistle and pop sounds warned her of another jolt. She fell. Eddie fired his laser too, and she dropped the gun.

Eddie scooped up the weapon as they ran out. "I'll take that."

The pair darted down the stairs and passed the Jamaican cleaner. "You can't be here," she shouted.

Rex and Eddie re-entered the arena. The Glasgow Smile was no longer on the floor. Fog machines filled the room with smoke as drum and bass blared out the speakers.

"We need to be quiet and stay in the shadows."

Rex gave a short nod. "Softly, softly, hidden dragon."

"It's softly, softly, *catchee monkey*. And in this case, I think we're the monkey."

They tiptoed down the corridor, Eddie's heart pumped fast. His head was light and woozy.

"Rex," he whispered. "I can't handle this. They could shoot from any direction."

"It's fine."

"But there are three of them. At least two guns. Remember how bad I lost last time."

"Just stick to what you're good at."

Eddie's eyes widened. "The only thing I'm good at in laser tag is getting shot."

Rex studied the arena. "Shh. To the right, in the corner, there's a shoulder sticking out."

"Nice catch."

Rex snuck a few steps forward and turned back to Eddie. "Thanks for taking me to laser tag."

Oh no, Eddie thought. *That's why he hasn't frozen. He thinks this is a game. Eddie couldn't explain it to Rex in case he froze.*

They tip-toed closer. Eddie pointed the real gun at the henchman's shoulder and snuck forward. Eddie's hand trembled. If he fired, the bullet could hit anything in a six-foot radius of the man's shoulder.

"I can't do it, Rex," he whispered.

Eddie turned around, and Rex was gone. He looked back at the henchman's shoulder and saw Rex sneak up from down the corridor. Rex had slipped around the arena and approached with his laser pointed at the henchman's back.

This is bad, he thought. *I've let Rex go out there against real gangsters, with real weapons, while he has a toy gun.*

Eddie shook his head at Rex and waved him back. Miming wasn't the most efficient form of communication, but it was all Eddie had.

Behind Rex, a shadow stepped out of the darkness. It was the third killer, a stocky man in a leather jacket with a handlebar moustache.

Eddie considered his options. If he didn't call out to warn Rex, his friend would be shot by the moustached man. If he did call out, then he'd alert the hiding henchman to Rex's whereabouts.

Above Eddie, he heard the footsteps of a heavy man. Through the metal grate flooring above, he saw the Glasgow Smile step over him. The Glasgow Smile stopped and looked down. He stared, but Eddie was hidden in the shadows. The assassin walked on.

Rex snuck closer to the hiding henchman, unaware the moustached man followed him. If Eddie warned Rex now, he would give himself away and be shot by the overhead villain.

In all the drama, Eddie forgot he had a real gun. Eddie stepped out from under the railing to get a clear shot of the Glasgow Smile above. As he stepped into the light, Eddie did a little sick in his mouth, but swallowed.

Like a real man, he told himself.

"Below you," a voice called out, it was Becky.

Eddie jumped out and fired at the Glasgow Smile. The scarred assassin shot back at Eddie but missed. Eddie jumped into another dark corner.

"Ah, my leg," the Glasgow Smile shouted.

Although Eddie aimed for the head, he still considered the shot a success. The hiding henchman scrambled towards Eddie's area, revealing bleach white hair that shone blue in the UV light. Rex fired his laser gun at the henchman's back and shocked him.

The white-haired man spun around and shot at Rex. Rex performed a drop and roll as he fired a laser at the moustached man behind him. Zapped, the moustached man's muscles spasmed, and he accidentally shot the white-haired man in the shoulder.

Rex dropped and rolled to the white-haired man and grabbed his laser gun. He shot a double round of lasers at the moustached man, shocking him enough to drop his pistol.

As Rex dropped and rolled down the hallway, the Glasgow Smile hobbled down the stairs and fired at Rex. Mid-roll, the bullet flew over Rex and landed in the moustached man's chest.

The white-haired man got up. With his working arm, he pointed his handgun at Rex. Grabbing the dead moustached man's gun, Rex shot with both the laser and the pistol. The laser triggered a zap, which threw the white-haired man's aim off, his gun fired at the corrugated metal wall. Rex's bullet hit the white-haired man's good shoulder. Both the henchman's wounded arms flopped as he fell to the ground.

Becky sprinted to the fire exit. The door flung open, and she skidded on the mop-soaked floor. She slipped and knocked herself out. In the hallway, the Jamaican cleaner tutted and returned to cleaning. The fire exit door swung back closed.

As Rex examined the real gun, the Glasgow Smile aimed at him. Eddie bolted over and whisked Rex behind a steel beam, as he ran his shoes bashed against the growing blisters.

"How come they got an upgraded weapon?" Rex said. "Did they pay extra to get one of those?"

"It's not a game, Rex."

"You're telling me. Anyone that thinks laser tag is a game doesn't respect—"

"It's real. This is all real."

Rex gasped. "What?"

The Glasgow Smile targeted his gun at Eddie's head.

"Real guns, real gangsters."

Horrified, Rex threw the gun on the floor. It hit the ground and fired. The bullet bounced off the gridded ceiling and into the head of the approaching Glasgow Smile. The assassin fell on his back with a thunk.

Rex and Eddie stood over him. His scars made him seem happy, as if he were having a wonderful dream.

"Rex, you did it."

"I did, didn't I. What did I do?"

"You fought, you didn't freeze."

Rex grinned. "I did?"

"You reacted, fight or flight."

"I shot a man!" Rex said, concerned.

"They're henchmen. You must have always wanted to shoot a henchman?"

"Oh, yeah, I guess so."

The siren blared, and the house lights flickered on. "Game over," the robotic announcer voice said.

"Game over indeed, boys," came the raspy voice of an old man. Between an entourage of heavies, a short man in his seventies stepped forward with the clip and clop of his brown chukka boots. It was Terry Palmer. "Game over indeed."

SEVENTEEN

The bags were removed from Rex and Eddie's heads. They were in an old disused warehouse, one of Palmer's many enterprises. Palmer walked up in his trademark boots, dry mud flaked from them as he got close. With each step he thumped his cane against the ground, causing the metal-plated bottom to chime.

"Do you know my name?" Palmer said. Rex and Eddie paused, wondering if it was a trick question. "Well, do you?"

"Terry Palmer," Eddie said.

"Do you know what they call me?"

Eddie looked down at his shoes. "Bootsy."

"Do you know why they call me Bootsy?"

Rex popped his head up. "I know. It's because you leave muddy footprints in The Octagon Shopping Centre."

Palmer sneered."You what?"

"Rex, be quiet."

"It's him. He's the muddy footprints at The Octagon."

"Rex, drop it."

"Where were you on the morning of Tuesday last week? Shopping I bet."

"I don't answer to you, boy."

"Show me the bottom of your boot," Rex said. "I bet it's the same print."

Palmer thumped his cane against the ground. "You listen to me. When you see the bottom of my boot, it'll be the last thing you see before I stomp your brains out. You understand?"

"Never mind," Rex said. "This isn't the right time."

Eddie breathed a sigh of relief.

"Now, do you know why they call me Bootsy?"

"Oh, I think I know," Rex said, excited to answer. If his hands weren't tied, he'd have raised one.

Palmer pointed at Rex. "Not you."

"Is it because you always wear them," Eddie said. "Even at your wedding."

"It's because when someone is of no use to me, I give them the boot. Are you boys of use to me?"

Rex and Eddie thought it over and shrugged their shoulders.

"Tell me where you kept the backup copies of Lawrence's manuscript."

"There, uh, isn't one," Eddie said.

"I see you've chosen to play this out to its logical conclusion," Palmer said. He turned to his men. "Get out the nail gun."

Eddie shuffled in his chair. "Why? What?"

"You want to play games. I've got the toys."

"I'm not playing. Tell him, Rex."

Rex shook his head. "We're not playing."

"Where are the copies?"

Eddie clenched his jaw. "There aren't any."

Rex nodded. "It's true."

"My boys searched every bit of paper in the Laser Flux office, and we didn't find it. Where did you put it?"

"Nowhere, we didn't have one."

"What did you go back there for then?"

"It's the only place we could think where a copy might exist. But we didn't put one there."

"I ain't buying it. You've got more than one copy. And it didn't go down in the fire."

Rex's phone rang. Palmer put his hand in Rex's pocket and grabbed the phone. He showed the calling number to Rex; Rex knew it was his nan. Palmer picked it up.

"Hello, Rex Milton's phone … Rex is a bit tied up at the moment … Will he be home late?" He eyeballed the pair. "I wouldn't expect him anytime soon."

Rex wiggled in his seat with panic. Palmer saw he'd rattled Rex and continued the call.

"You want him to know your prescription is ready for collection … I can have someone pick that up for you, darling. What's your address?"

Rex hopped in his chair as a henchman covered his mouth.

"Lovely. Eight Perrin Street? I'll see if I can get one of my boys to do it for you … Of course, they'll go to the pharmacy first." Terry looked at Rex and shook his head.

"And it's to pick up Quinapril? Is that the orange one?" he asked with interest. "Yeah, I take that one too, but I have to take the anti-dizziness one with it. The blue ones? … No, I tried the yellow and it didn't work … You should ask your doctor to change."

The Henchmen's faces glazed over, like they'd heard his medication talk far too often.

"Anyway, I got to go love. Goodbye." Palmer hung up the phone. "Your nan says her prescription's ready. If you don't start talking, you can pick it up," he raised his voice, "while you get the doctor to fix the amount of holes I'm gonna leave in you."

"I know what this looks like," Eddie said. "That we're lying, and you need to torture us to get the truth, but we're telling you the truth right now."

Palmer's nostrils flared. "What kind of idiot doesn't make copies?"

"Us idiots," Eddie said. "Please, this is our first case."

Rex nodded. "We don't know the rules."

Palmer stepped closer and examined them. He stood up straight and sighed.

"I believe you," he said. Rex and Eddie relaxed. "But I can't have people think I've gone soft. Get to work fellas."

Two heavies grabbed the backs of their chairs and dragged the pair closer to the power sockets. The chairs screeched along the warehouse floor, metal against concrete.

"And next time," Palmer shouted, "bring the battery-powered nail gun. I hate that noise. I'll be back in a minute." Palmer walked through the double doors.

The taller heavy with an egg-shaped head plugged in the nail gun. "Who wants to go first?"

"I'll go first," Rex said.

He pointed the gun at Rex's foot.

"No, it should be me," Eddie said. The egghead aimed the nail gun at Eddie's foot.

"That's kind of you, but I should have made the copies."

"That's true, but I still insist I go first."

The egghead moved the gun between Rex and Eddie as they spoke.

"No, me," Rex said, "I got you to start up the detective agency."

"That's also true, but you're my best friend, and I insist I go first."

Rex nodded. "Okay, then. You can go first."

The egghead settled the gun in Eddie's direction.

Eddie stiffened. "Wait, what?"

"You insisted."

"Yeah, because it was the honourable thing to do."

"Yes, you're very honourable." Rex turned to the egghead. "He's the most honourable man I know."

"Well, I didn't think that would be the last word on the matter."

"We should hurry this up," Rex said to the egghead. "You're making him anxious."

"I take it back. Rex should go first."

"But you said, you'd go first. You can't take that back."

"You took yours back."

"No, you took mine. I just agreed with you."

The egghead let the nail gun hover over Eddie's foot as they argued.

Eddie tucked his chin."Hey, why are you resting that thing on me."

Jim Jams woke from a power-nap induced by fifteen minutes of yoga stretches and a lavender tea. He checked his phone and found a message from Rex. The text read, *Gonna raid laser flux for evidence. Should get some good shooting in too if you're interested.*

Jim Jams was interested. He'd have to take a bus to Laser Flux, but he'd get to be the hero that came in at the last minute. He packed his supplies: a bottle of Scotch, five cigarettes, a packet of Tic Tacs, his Caffe Nero rewards card, and a Yorkie chocolate bar for emergencies.

Outside Laser Flux, Jim Jams saw two heavies escort Rex and Eddie into a black SUV with bags on their heads. He recognised the pair by their walks. Eddie took hesitant steps, but Rex maintained his dainty skip, even when strong-armed with a bag on his head.

Jim Jams found the Morris Minor parked outside. He hot-wired the car and followed the black SUV into the countryside. For a while, he thought he saw a moped gang in the rear-mirror follow him. Although he usually fasted in the mid-afternoon, Jim Jams decided he had paranoia brought on by a sugar crash and ate the emergency Yorkie.

The Black SUV pulled up outside a warehouse in Snodling village. Jim Jams watched the two heavies drag Rex and Eddie inside. He approached the warehouse on foot and snuck along the building's side. On the corner, he found a small bathroom window ajar. He hopped up to grab the ledge and lifted himself up, which was somewhat easy thanks to his yoga regime.

Jim Jams pushed his head and chest through the window. Before he could drop into the bathroom, the door swung open and Terry Palmer entered. Jim Jams kicked his legs out to pin himself in place while his full torso hung into the men's room. The old man walked straight past the hovering head of Jim Jams and relieved himself at the urinal. Jim Jams waited in silence as the old man peed. Palmer's troubled prostate made him grunt and growl, which Jim Jams found quite off-putting.

Palmer finished up and headed to the sink. Jim Jams noticed his own reflection in the mirror and straightened his back. He lifted his whole upper body out of the mirror's view with just the strength of his core. If he dropped even a little, Palmer would see his reflection. The old man gave his hands a good scrub and looked in the mirror. In the reflection's upper right corner he noticed a twinkle. It was a medallion hanging from Jim Jams's gold necklace. Palmer turned and glared at Jim Jams.

Panicked, Jim Jams backed out of the window. His rocking hips knocked the handle holding the window open; the window fell and pinned him in place.

Palmer twisted the handle of his cane and spun it a few times. He pulled the handle up, revealing a sword hidden inside the cane. Palmer pointed it at Jim Jams's gut, and walked forward. Jim Jams jumped, pushed and pulled, but his hips were wedged in the window frame. The old man drove the blade through Jim Jams belly like a skewer.

Jim Jams let out a high pitch scream.

EIGHTEEN

The egghead pointed the nail gun at Eddie's foot and placed his finger on the trigger when Jim Jams's scream echoed through the warehouse floor. The egghead and the short heavy marched to the bathroom to check on their boss. For a brief few moments, Rex and Eddie were alone.

Eddie wriggled his chair. "Rex, can you move?"

"A little."

"Rock closer to me."

As the pair rocked back and forth, the chairs crawled a few millimetres at a time.

"We need to untie ourselves," Eddie said.

"How?"

The pair viewed the nail gun. It wasn't an ideal situation, but they needed to work with what they had. Both rocked their chairs until they fell on their side. Eddie kicked back against the wall and grabbed the nail gun behind him.

"Point your back to my back," Eddie said. "I'll get close

and shoot the nail at the rope between your hands. It should cut the rope. Then you can untie me."

"What if you miss?" Rex said.

Both knew the answer: one of Rex's hands would be nailed to the chair, or his backside.

Eddie forced an assuring smile. "I won't. It'll be easy."

Rex and Eddie moved back-to-back as Eddie tried to position the nail gun. He pulled the nail gun closer, but the power cable had no slack.

"Give me the gun," Rex said. "I'm closer."

"I can make it work. We just need to rock closer to the wall."

"Eddie, it's fine. I'll shoot your ropes, and we'll be good to go."

Eddie ignored Rex and tried to push the chair closer.

"They're gonna walk back in any second."

"Fine." Eddie slid the nail gun over. "You're sure you can do this?"

"Of course."

As they were both back-to-back, Rex felt the gun and ropes in search of a sweet spot between Eddie's wrists.

"Here?"

"Left a little."

"Here?"

Beads of sweat rolled down Eddie's forehead. "I can feel it there … still feel it … that's good, no wait. Okay, go ahead."

They both closed their eyes and held their breath. Rex fired the nail.

"Ahhh!" Jim Jams screamed as Palmer pulled the blade out of his belly.

The egghead and the short heavy burst in.

"Get him," Palmer shouted. The two henchmen yanked Jim Jams by the arms into the men's room.

Jim Jams expected to be more upset at the sight of his blood leaking on the floor. He was surprised it didn't hurt all that much. The thin blade only touched the nerve endings of his skin while his insides didn't feel a thing. He wondered if doing yoga on the bus beforehand helped him keep calm.

"Who are you?" Palmer demanded.

"Jim Jams."

"What?"

"Jim Jams."

"What are you saying to me?" Palmer turned to the heavies. "I don't understand what anyone under thirty says anymore."

"I'm thirty-two," Jim Jams said.

"You better grow up then. Dressed like a Village People pirate, I don't get it. Take him in with the others."

Eddie breathed a sigh of relief. The nail clearly shot through the ropes and partly sliced it.

Rex edged closer. "I'll cut the rope this time. Ready, Eddie?"

"No, wait. I can break free."

"Are you sure? I've got plenty more nails?"

Eddie pulled a hand free from the ropes. He tugged hard enough to give him a rope burn. With both hands able, he freed himself and untied Rex's feet.

The sharp thunk of Palmer's cane hitting the floor grew louder with each step.

"He's coming," Rex said.

Eddie pulled Rex's chair up and covered his feet with the loose rope.

Rex looked confused. "What are you doing?"

Eddie settled back into his chair and hid his hands behind it.

Palmer entered while his heavies dragged Jim Jams in.

"This one of your friends?"

Rex nodded while Eddie bounced his head to suggest "sort of."

"Who else knows you're here?"

"No-one," Eddie said.

Palmer pointed at Eddie. "Nail his balls to the chair."

The egghead pointed the nail gun at Eddie's crotch. Eddie leapt up from the chair a second before the nail was fired. The nail embedded in the chair between his standing legs.

Eddie grabbed the chair and hit the egghead's skull with it. The egghead fell to the ground. Rex jumped to his feet, with his hands still tied to the chair, and charged at the short heavy. The heavy pulled a gun as Rex knocked him to the ground. Rex stomped on the man's hand until he dropped the gun and kicked the weapon towards Jim Jams.

The egghead laid unconscious, but Eddie hit him with the chair a few more times for good measure, and pulled a gun from the henchman's inner jacket. Jim Jams and Eddie both pointed their weapons at Palmer.

"Am I supposed to be scared?" he said.

"How come I don't have a weapon?" Rex asked, while loosening himself from the chair.

"You're fine," Eddie said.

"How am I fine? I got a baddy right here." Rex pointed at the short heavy.

"Here." Eddie threw him the nail gun. Rex grabbed

the nail gun at the handle, and accidentally fired a nail into Eddie's thigh.

Eddie let out a bloody scream.

"Sorry, Eddie."

"You idiot."

"I said I was sorry."

"That really hurts, Rex."

"Again I'm sorry. But I bet it distracts from your blisters?"

"Rex. Don't."

Palmer looked over to Jim Jams. "Are they always like this?"

Jim Jams shrugged his shoulders.

"I'll make it up to you," Rex said.

"How?"

Rex pointed the nail gun at the short heavy's thigh and fired. The heavy screamed and wailed.

Eddie gawked. "What did you do that for?"

"To make things even."

"How is that even?"

"Well, I made it a draw. One all."

"Except my nail is a home goal."

"I'm sorry, okay," Rex yelled. He squeezed the handle without thinking, shooting another nail. Everyone flinched. The nail landed a few inches from Palmer's foot.

Rex winced. "My bad."

Palmer raised his hands. "Someone get that thing off him."

Eddie nodded. "Jim Jams, take the nail gun."

"But—" Rex said.

"Quiet, Rex. Jim Jams is in charge of the nail gun from now on."

Jim Jams dragged himself on the floor a foot and gave

up. "I'm a bit busy bleeding through my favourite shirt, thank you very much."

"Fine, you can hold the nail gun as long as it's not plugged in."

"What if the baddy moves?" Rex said.

"You've already nailed his leg to the floor."

"He's got hands."

Eddie waved his gun. "Excuse me, henchman. Are you going to move?"

The short heavy shook his head rapidly.

Palmer swiped the sword from his cane.

Eddie pointed his gun back at Palmer. "Really?"

Palmer chucked the sword on the floor. "How about we settle this like men?" He raised his fists.

"Um, I think I'll stick with the gun, thanks."

Officer Sumner scratched his head with the end of his pen. In his mid-forties, Sumner was a friendly man with bright eyes and laughter lines. As a local policeman, he usually dealt with village issues like a dispute between two neighbours regarding an overgrown hedge. Now he stood in a warehouse questioning two baby-faced private detectives as his colleagues cuffed the notorious Terry Palmer and his two bodyguards.

Officer Sumner checked his notes. "So the charges are two counts of murder, two counts of kidnapping, police corruption, attempted murder, arson, two counts of grievous bodily harm?"

"Two?" Jim Jams asked while being put on an ambulance stretcher.

"Yeah," Rex said with shifty eyes. "They shot Eddie in the leg with a nail gun."

"Oh, right," Jim Jams said as the ambulance driver pushed him to the warehouse exit.

"We're going to get you a blood transfusion," the driver told Jim Jams.

"It's all right, fella. I just need two shots of whiskey, one shot of wheatgrass, a ciggie, one coconut water, and half a Mars bar."

Sumner put away his notes. "Well, I've got plenty of questions for the pair of you. How about we get your nail wound seen to and head to the station?"

Rex raised his hand. "How do we know Palmer hasn't bought you off?"

Officer Sumner laughed. "I'm not sure what happens in Cloisterham, but we don't have many dealings with gangsters out here. Why, it's been three months since a reported robbery, and that was a pet tortoise."

"Did you catch him?" Eddie asked.

"No need. The thief returned the tortoise with an apology taped to the shell."

At the Snodling Police Station's interview room Rex and Eddie took Officer Sumner through their adventure, point by point.

"How do you boys like your tea?"

"Just milk, no sugar, thanks," Eddie said.

"Do you have a slice of lemon?" Rex asked.

"I'm afraid not."

"Same as Eddie then."

Sumner turned to the bearded policeman that stood by the door. "Will you get these men a cup of tea and make a photocopy of this please?" Sumner handed the policeman his notes.

"What about Becky Cooper?" Eddie said.

"We've found her flight booking for Jamaica and the authorities will rendezvous with her at the airport check-in."

"What's gonna happen to Palmer?" Rex said.

"Not sure. We can charge him for stabbing a sword into Mr James Jams, but since he broke and entered into Palmer's property, it won't hold up. Unless we can connect him to the men that attacked you at Laser Flux that will get dropped too."

Eddie's body tightened. "But he murdered his brother."

"And you say the only evidence was burned."

Rex nodded. "Twice."

"But what about Derek Lawrence?"

"Again, the documents were the only thing that would suggest the intent to kill Lawrence. And even then, it would be a hired hand. So it's hard to connect him."

Eddie sat back in a sulk. "You don't believe us."

"Oh, I believe you. But if I haven't got anything to convince a judge and jury, then there's no point."

The bearded officer returned with the papers.

"I meant two copies."

The bearded officer offered his hand. "Sorry. I'll take it back and do another."

Sumner shook his head. "Press copy and then select the previous scan. It does a copy from memory."

Rex sat up straight. "You can do that?"

"Yes."

"Eddie, we can get the evidence."

Eddie sat up too. "You made the copies with the neighbouring office's copier."

"Yes."

Sumner grinned. "Well, lads. Let's see if we can get those papers."

NINETEEN

Officer Sumner and Rex stood outside 369 High Street as Eddie unlocked the front door. They ran upstairs and found the fire damage was contained to their office alone. Harold exited another unit with his cleaning cart.

"Harold," Eddie said. "You have to let us into next door's office. Please."

They explained the details, and after some hesitation, Harold unlocked the office. At the printer Rex pressed copy and the display message updated: *No document found. Check Again?*

Eddie slumped. "This one doesn't do it."

"Sorry, lads," Officer Sumner said.

Rex examined the printer. His head hovered a few inches from the machine. After inspection, he pressed an arrow key. A new option came up: *Print from previous scan?*

"Rex, you're a genius."

"Fingers crossed the printer hasn't been used since." Rex pressed the copy button and paper fed through the machine. Anticipation built as the printer head slid back and forth. The printer pushed out a sheet of paper.

Rex grabbed the paper and stared at the result.

"Well, what is it?" Officer Sumner said.

Rex revealed the copy. A black and white scan of a bare bottom.

"It's not a total loss," Rex said. "At least we know what the cute girl in the office's bum looks like."

Eddie read the printer display: *Copy again?*

He pressed the left arrow key to search for a previous option: Print from previous scan? He pushed the right arrow which revealed a list of five times and dates.

"I think I've got it. Rex, when did you make the copies?"

"Uh, it would have been two days ago. I did it about eleven p.m."

Eddie scrolled back two days and pressed copy. The first sheet printed.

"My turn." Overwhelmed with nerves, Eddie grabbed the sheet and read.

"Well?" Officer Sumner said.

Eddie turned the page over to reveal the P&P Publishing acceptance letter. "We have the evidence."

The machine printed out every piece of paper Rex had copied.

"You did it, Rex. You saved us."

"No problem, give us a hug."

Eddie's shoulders hunched up. "I'm not a hugger."

Rex opened his arms. "Come on, bring it in."

"We should get this to the police station."

"Okay, but then we hug."

Rex, Eddie, and Officer Sumner walked by the burnt out office unit. Eddie pushed the door open, and all three took a peek inside. The floor and walls were a charcoal colour, and the crispy furniture lay in pieces.

Officer Sumner tapped the door. "Come on lads, let's not dwell."

"I bet the papers went up fast," Eddie said.

Thunk. Officer Sumner took a knock to the head and fell to the ground.

"It was a pretty clean job," said a voice from behind Rex and Eddie. Brown stepped in with a gun pointed at the pair.

Eddie stomped his right foot. "You've got to be joking."

"Hand over the papers."

Rex shrugged his shoulders. "What papers?"

"I heard everything from the hallway. Hand it over."

Rex shook his head and clutched the documents.

Eddie raised his hands. "Rex, don't get shot."

"You want to listen to your friend."

"If we give him the papers he's not gonna shoot us, there's another policeman waiting in the car outside. He'll hear it."

"I'll shoot if I have too."

Rex backed up another step. "I don't like you. You're a bad man."

"Hand over the papers."

With a pouted lip, Rex pulled out the copies and reached them out. Brown grabbed the other end and pulled it. Rex wouldn't loosen his grip.

"Hand it over now."

"Rex, drop it."

"Give it," Brown barked.

Rex let go a split-second before Brown gave a big yank. Brown fell back a step.

Rex grinned. "Smooth."

Brown regained his footing. "Now, where were we?" He put his hand in his jacket pocket and pulled out a silencer.

Eddie rolled his eyes. "Perfect." He was pretty scared the first time his life was in danger, at this point it was an irritating inconvenience. "Just bloody perfect."

Brown screwed the silencer on.

"Eddie," Rex said.

"What?"

"I could really do with a hug."

Eddie sighed. "Fine."

"You've got ten seconds," Brown said.

Eddie walked up to Rex's embrace when the door knocked three times. Brown stepped to the window and checked the police car; the other officer was still inside the vehicle.

The door opened and Harold barged in. He grabbed Brown by the throat. Panicked, Brown fired two bullets into the roof. The already fire-damaged ceiling dropped a hefty chunk of plaster on both the fighting men.

"What the hell is going on here?" Eddie said.

Rex's eyes flashed. "Harold's the Door Knock Killer."

"Don't be ridiculous."

A third and fourth shot fired into the office window, leaving two neat holes joined together by a crack. Rex and Eddie ducked behind the blackened desk while the two men wrestled on the floor.

"I'm telling you, he's the Door Knock Killer. He knocked, he's trying to kill someone. What more do you need?"

"You're delusional." Eddie remembered the details: Harold was easily annoyed by mess, he liked to clean things up so why not people? He had a wheelbarrow to move bodies around in. He remembered Harold's words when they looked through the wheelie bin, "You're gonna get me in trouble."

Is that why I thought I saw Rex drop into the bin men's lorry? he thought.

"Hey Harold, are you the Door Knock Killer?" Rex said.

Harold bobbed his head left to right. "That's a bit too sensationalist for my liking. The tabloids paint an ugly picture." He gave Brown a few punches in between strangling him.

"Are we meant to stop him?" Rex said.

"I think so."

Brown pushed the old man off and pulled his gun on Harold. Harold backed away. Brown shooed Rex and Eddie with the weapon, and they stepped back with their hands up.

Rex, Eddie, and Harold were at the mercy of Brown.

"I've got two bullets left, so you're gonna have to pair up. Who wants to go in front?"

Rex stepped forward. "Me."

"Well, we should talk about this first," Eddie said.

"Okay, you."

"No, I mean, I just don't want to be hasty."

Rex shrugged. "I'm easy, which do you want?"

"I just wanted to talk about it."

"Come on you two," Brown said. "Stop making every. Little. Thing. So. Hard."

"I'm not fond of the front," Eddie said. "But I don't want people to think I used you as a human shield."

"What if," Rex said, "I took the bullet for you? Like he was gonna shoot you, and I got in the way. You won't look like a coward, and I get to be a bit of a hero."

Eddie nodded. "That could work. But how do we make sure people know that?"

"Excuse me, Mister Detective Man."

Brown pursed his lips. "What now?"

"If people ask will you tell them I heroically jumped in the way and took the bullet?"

"Fine."

Rex took a diving pose with one leg in the air. He pulled a face like he was already shot. "I'm ready."

Brown took a step back to aim, and the floorboard beneath him gave out. He pulled his foot from the hole and tripped backwards. Brown hit the window with the back of his head. Already cracked by Brown's bullets, the window-pane shattered.

Harold kicked the burnt rubbish basket at Brown, and he dropped out the window. Brown fired his last two bullets as he fell out of view.

Feeling impatient, Rex opened one eye. "Did I miss something?"

Rex and Eddie peered out the broken window. On the street below, they saw Brown's dead body in a pool of blood. Next to Brown stood a wide-eyed Tim with his moped gang; they followed the pair since they saw Jim Jams drive by in the Morris Minor. Tim looked up at Rex and Eddie with his mouth agape.

"Who wants to go next?" Rex shouted.

Tim and the gang ran off. The detective pair grinned.

"Nice one, Rex."

On the office floor, Harold spat up blood. He'd taken both shots. Rex rushed over, kneeled down, and held Harold's head to comfort the old psychopath. Eddie stood back knowing there was nothing he could do.

"Why'd you kill all those people?" Rex said.

Harold groaned. "Cloisterham … an okay place to live."

Eddie kneeled. "Why did you save us?"

Harold tried to answer but coughed.

"Is it because we give you renewed hope in humanity?" Rex offered. "Do we remind you of one of your kids? Do you believe we can make a difference in the world?"

"Nah, I just hate coppers." Harold's head collapsed, he was dead.

Eddie turned to Rex. "Well, it was still nice of him."

TWENTY

Rex poured water over Officer Sumner's head to wake him up. Before Sumner could stand Eddie handed over the evidence copies. Sumner promised it was enough to send Terry Palmer to court and start a proper investigation.

Although it wasn't enough to pin the two murders on Palmer, it warranted a search of his home, which brought up enough evidence to put him in jail for tax evasion and owning illegal weapons.

Since the whole thing was a setup, there was no five grand reward. Rex and Eddie were still broke. Eddie arranged an overdraft with the bank to tide him over. He withdrew enough pound coins to pay back Billy the Quid.

They found Billy on the High Street, milking his arm sling for all it was worth.

"I got your pound coins, Billy."

"Don't worry, mate. I get more money now I'm wounded. Got a fiver?"

Eddie gave him a fiver and kept the coins.

Rex and Eddie both visited The Octagon Shopping

Centre. Rex gave Griffin one of Palmer's muddy boots and announced, "The dirty footprint culprit is in jail, Chief. No need to thank me, justice is my thanks. Let's just forget everything that happened and go our separate ways."

Griffin's forehead wrinkled. "What are you talking about?"

"Exactly, Chief. Exactly."

Eddie entered the shoe shop and approached Melinda.

"I'm sorry I messed up our date."

"I read you caught a murderer."

"Two murderers, actually. One of them was a serial killer, but I don't like to brag." Eddie plonked his shoes on the counter. "I'd like to return these. I tried to break them in, but they just hurt all the time."

Melinda picked up a shoe. Paint, bloodstains, scuffs, scratches, and marks covered the shoe.

"They look lived in."

"All in a day's work solving murders."

"You really went out and got what you wanted, didn't you?"

"Yeah." Eddie took a moment while Melinda processed the return. "Actually, I don't know what I'm doing, and for the first time, I'm fine with that." He signed for the balance to be put back on his card. "Goodbye, Melinda."

Eddie joined Rex at the office to drop off his key. He only agreed to do the one case to get his investment back. Now they had no money and no case.

The building's insurance paid for the office to be fixed up and repainted.

"The place is in brilliant shape," Eddie told Rex.

"They even installed a new window. Watch this." Rex

ran over to open and close the window. "How luxurious is that?"

"Nice. Well, Rex. This is it."

"What are you going to do?"

"Not sure, I might do some pizza deliveries with the Morris Minor. I've got just enough cash to get new headlights and fix the ignition after Jim Jams hot-wired it. How is Jim Jams?"

"He's well happy," Rex said. "Every night he shows girls his new scars, tells them a different story about it each time. Last night involved a burning orphanage."

Eddie grinned. "I'm glad he got something out of the experience."

"How can you go back to normal life after the adventure we just had?"

"Oh, it's quite easy," Eddie said.

"But look," Rex held up a copy of The Kent Gazette. The headline read, *Two Locals Capture Door Knock Killer.* "We're heroes."

"It's not quite true though, is it?"

"No, but I did work out Harold was the Door Knock Killer."

"By watching him knock on a door and try to kill a man, it's hardly detective work."

Rex smiled. "Well, I'm taking the credit. One thing has been bothering me though."

"What?"

"Who exactly did kill Derek Lawrence? I know they worked for Palmer, but who were they?"

Eddie smiled. "Becky said she thought it was the bouncer who hired her, but I guess we'll never know."

"I thought maybe the Glasgow Smile, but Brown knew his way around here. And the egg-headed man had the eyes of a killer and—"

"Rex," Eddie said. "You're doing a little dance."

"I know, I got to go to the bathroom, but I'm excited."

"Just go to the toilet."

"Fine, but don't leave until I'm back and ready for my goodbye hug."

"There isn't gonna be a—"

Rex left before Eddie could finish. Eddie sighed, placed his key on the new desk, and headed to the door. The office phone rang and Eddie picked it up.

"Hello, uh, Milton Miles Investigations."

"Hi, yes, I'm looking for a detective. Are you the men who solved the Door Knock Killer mystery?"

"I, uh, yes. I am."

"Great, I believe I have a corporate spy. I need someone to debug the office of surveillance equipment. Are you available?"

"Well, I'm actually going to have to pass but my partner—"

"Oh no, I need the pair of you. I want the best men for the job; We'll pay handsomely."

A red light blinked on the phone.

"Could you excuse me while I put you on hold for one minute?" Eddie pressed the button. "Hello, Milton Miles Investigations."

"Hi, my brother's been acting suspicious, and I'm worried about him. Could I hire you to follow him for a few days, see what he's been up to?"

"I'm sure we can sort something out, my business partner can get back to you?" Another red light blinked. "Please hold. Hello, Milton Miles Investigations."

"Can I speak to Milton or Miles please?"

"This is Eddie Miles."

"I've lost my cat and was wondering if you would be able to look for her?"

"I don't think we do pets, but I'll ask my business partner about it."

Red bulbs lit up the phone as Rex came back in the room.

"Rex, can you take this call while I get some stationery to write on, we got two, no, three cases."

Rex smiled. "Certainly."

Eddie picked up his key as Rex grabbed the phone.

"See you soon, Eddie."

"Yeah, see you soon, partner."

Rex held the receiver to his head. "Milton Miles Investigations. You spy with our little eye."

Rex & Eddie return in

FELINE FATALE

GET A FREE BOOK!

One of the best things about writing is building a relationship with my readers. I occasionally send newsletters with details on new releases, special offers, and other news related to the Rex & Eddie Mysteries series.

When you sign up to my newsletter, I'll send you ***Rebels Without A Claus: A Rex & Eddie Mystery***, a novelette set between book 1 and book 2!

Get your freebie today by signing up at

WWW.SEAN-CAMERON.COM/FREEBOOK

ENJOY THIS BOOK?

YOU CAN MAKE A BIG DIFFERENCE!

Book reviews are an excellent tool for getting the attention of new readers. If you've enjoyed *Catchee Monkey* I would be very grateful if you could spend just five minutes leaving an honest review (it can be as short as you like) on the book's Amazon page.

Thank you very much.

ABOUT THE AUTHOR

Sean Cameron is from Rochester, England and currently lives in Los Angeles, California. When not laughing at the British weather report, he finds time to write the comedy book series *Rex & Eddie Mysteries.*

He likes carrot cake, dinosaurs, and hiking; although not much hiking happens as he fears being eaten by a mountain lion. He dislikes squash soup, traffic, and mountain lions.

You can drop him an email at sean@sean-cameron.com or visit his online home at www.sean-cameron.com.

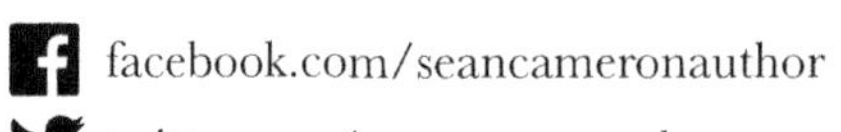
facebook.com/seancameronauthor

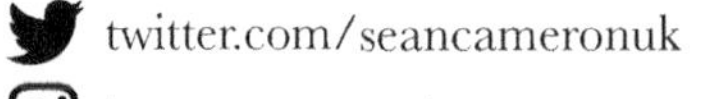
twitter.com/seancameronuk

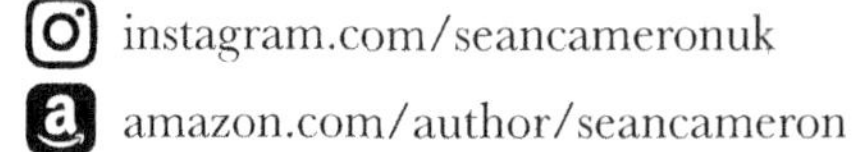
instagram.com/seancameronuk

amazon.com/author/seancameron

ALSO BY SEAN CAMERON

Catchee Monkey: A Rex & Eddie Mystery (Book 1)

Amateur sleuths Rex and Eddie stumble upon a murder mystery that sees them outnumbered, outgunned, and outwitted. They'll have to solve the case before it kills them or before they end up killing each other. *Catchee Monkey* is a hilarious detective novella that's equal parts British Comedy and gripping thriller.

Feline Fatale: A Rex & Eddie Mystery (Book 2)

Rex and Eddie accept a case to find the missing cat of their old school teacher and first crush, Mrs Nerdlinger. The duo are pitted against a creepy stalker, a nosey neighbour, and a rude old woman claiming to be the cat's real owner. *Feline Fatale* is a fun and farcical thriller full of sharp dialogue, clever twists, and silly antics.

The Office Spy: A Rex & Eddie Mystery (Book 3)

Spies, sleuths, and sandwich thieves — For Rex and Eddie, it's just another day in the office. Hired to find a corporate spy, Rex and Eddie go undercover as pest exterminators. Their spy hunting antics entangle the pair in office politics, employee secrets, and the search for the kitchen's sandwich thief. *The Office Spy* is a fun novella packed with silly hijinks, clever jokes, and crazy thrills.

The Third Banana: A Rex & Eddie Mystery (Book 4)

After a routine surveillance job ends in witnessing a kidnapping, dimwitted detectives Rex and Eddie get on the wrong side of super sleuth Jason Cole. He's special forces, they're just… special. Now the detective duo must prove their worth against the best, solve the kidnapping case, and stop a gang turf war that could destroy their hometown. Full of witty mayhem, *The Third Banana* is a comedy thriller with appeal.

ACKNOWLEDGMENTS

I'd like to thank the following for their help with this book: Thea Green and Julian Maurer.

Printed in Great Britain
by Amazon